Samuel maneuvered his bulk out of the cave and turned around to pull Maggie through.

They looked around.

They had come out in a heavily wooded area, and Samuel knew this wasn't where they needed to be. "The exit must be farther up." He put his hands on his hips, disappointment extinguishing his confidence.

"It's okay. Let's just get back in and keep walking." The strained optimism in Maggie's voice didn't disguise her anxiety. "It can't be much farther. Right?"

"Right." Samuel hoped he sounded convincing. For a moment they considered the tunnel, loath to leave the sunlight for its dim interior. With a sigh, Maggie wordlessly strode back over and slipped back inside. Samuel was close behind when he heard the sharp intake of her breath.

"Sam!"

He nearly dove back inside the tunnel. It took a second for his eyes to adjust, even with the aid of the headlamp, but he felt fear grip his chest once he knew what he was seeing.

Two masked men flanked Maggie, one with a gun trained on her, the other with a gun pointed right at his head...

Leah Conte considers herself a world citizen; she was raised in New Zealand but has also lived in Australia, Southeast Asia, East Africa and now the USA. While completing her master's degree in education, she turned to writing as a creative outlet. Now, in between teaching and raising her three children, she gets to write stories she loves...and she hopes you will love them, too!

Books by Leah Conte

Love Inspired Suspense

Exposing Killer Secrets

Visit the Author Profile page at LoveInspired.com.

EXPOSING KILLER SECRETS

LEAH CONTE

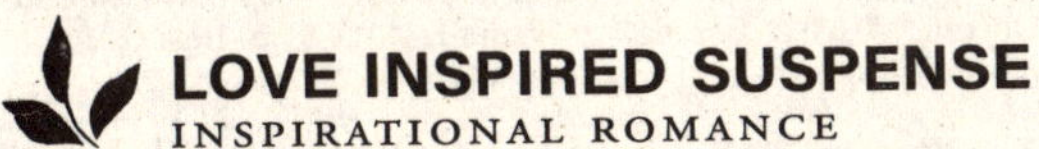

Recycling programs for this product may not exist in your area.

ISBN-13: 978-1-335-95762-7

Exposing Killer Secrets

Love Inspired
22 Adelaide St. West, 41st Floor
Toronto, Ontario M5H 4E3, Canada
www.LoveInspired.com

HarperCollins Publishers
Macken House, 39/40 Mayor Street Upper,
Dublin 1, D01 C9W8, Ireland
www.HarperCollins.com

Printed in Lithuania

And all things, whatsoever ye shall ask in prayer,
believing, ye shall receive.
—*Matthew* 21:22

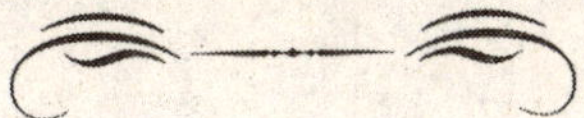

For Kelly, who always knew this was possible.

ONE

Silence hung in the air, but Maggie Dalton knew not to trust it. She froze in the middle of the public restroom, her eyes laser focused on the doorknob that had just been rattling. Her ears were attuned to the shuffling she'd heard outside the door. The tiny bathroom she had stopped at was very basic and, since it was the offseason and there were no tourists around, it was deserted. She had been driving from Los Angeles for nearly two days, and she managed to get on the last vehicle ferry to Vargo Island from thc Washington mainland. Aftcr driving off the ferry, she had decided to wash up before getting a few hours of sleep in her car.

The door handle wiggled again. The simple knob lock keeping the door fastened wouldn't hold up under pressure. "It's occupied!" Maggie shouted, a note of fear permeating her words. She heard the sound of feet moving outside on the cement path, and then the doorknob jostled again. Who could be trying to get into the restroom? She hadn't thought to check if any other cars were parked around the rest stop before she went in. She scolded herself for leaving her phone in the car, but even if she'd had it on her, should she call the police? She thought back to the cryptic message she had received a couple of days ago from a blocked number.

Text this number when you get to Vargo Island. Do not tell anyone that you are coming here. Do not trust ANYONE in this town. They are probably in on the cover-up, too. If you want to find out the truth about Carlie, come alone and keep your mouth shut. And don't expect this to be easy.

It was the latest in a string of messages she'd received from a contact she'd made on an online crime message board. This mystery person claimed to have important information about Carlie's death. Maggie had no reason to trust this source, yet it was her only link to Carlie—apart from the single piece of evidence she'd managed to secure.

She had to try to get out of this herself. She looked around wildly as a loud thud made the door shake. The room was bare except for the toilet, a sink and a plunger beside the toilet. She grasped the wooden shaft of the plunger and held it in front of her, then almost began laughing. What was she possibly going to do with this? Fashion it into a shiv?

All thoughts of mirth were wiped from her mind with the next crash against the door. Whoever was on the other side was obviously ramming it with their shoulder—and by the sounds of the impacts, that person was strong. With the next collision, Maggie heard the wood in the frame splinter and crack. Her heart was pounding as she did something she hadn't done in a long time. She began to pray. *Dear Lord, please be with me at this moment. Guide my next steps. Protect me.*

She looked around again and froze as she took in the small rectangular window set above the sink. The sun had set hours ago, but motion sensor security lights outside the building illuminated the parking lot. Her car was parked right on the other side of the window. If she could climb out somehow, maybe it would give her an extra minute to make it to her car and get away. She had to try.

Maggie threw the plunger aside, then clambered nimbly onto the sink, silently thanking God for the strength of her body, built from her many years of dance classes. She unfastened the window just as she heard a wrenching groan from the door. It was beginning to break, and she knew she was nearly out of time. The window was small, but she thought she could just squeeze through. It was her only option.

The screeching of splintering wood was louder now. She pushed the window hard and breathed a sigh of relief that it swung all the way open, the latch mechanism obviously not working. She grasped on to the frame with both hands just as a loud crash erupted from the front door. The lock had finally broken and the door swung open with a tremendous bang.

She froze as she looked over her shoulder to see a black-clothed figure looming in the door. His face was largely obscured by a hood and gaiter mask, but his eyes found hers from across the room. They were eerily blue and devoid of emotion. Terror sent goosebumps erupting along her arms. Time had seemed to slow down—

she paused for maybe two seconds, but it felt like hours. Maggie's heart was pounding furiously. She leveraged her head, then torso out the window, wriggling desperately as her hips stuck in the frame. *Lord be with me! Please help me.* She prayed desperately and redoubled her efforts despite the screaming protests of her muscles. Suddenly she felt gloved hands grip her ankles like a vise.

"Get back here!" a gruff voice shouted. She screamed and braced herself against his grasp, kicking wildly. Even as she screamed, she knew there was no one around to hear her. She had taken the last ferry to Vargo, and she had been the only one on it.

"Let me go!" Maggie screeched, pulling with all her strength to try and get through the window. She could feel splinters of wood worm their way under her skin as her hands desperately scrabbled against the window frame, trying to find further purchase.

"You should never have come back here! There was nothing you could do for her then, and we're not going to let you poke your nose in now!" the man yelled. A shudder went through Maggie's body. She knew her assailant must have something to do with Carlie's death and with the texts she had been receiving. That voice was rapidly drowned out as her survival instincts erased any other thoughts.

She desperately searched the gloom outside, trying to see if there was anyone who could help her, but the area was deserted. Just as she felt he was about to pull her back in, her foot connected with his chin. He let out a cry and released one of her ankles. Knowing this was her last chance, she summoned all her energy and kicked out furiously. She heard him wail in pain as the heel of her shoe smashed against what she assumed was his nose, and the force propelled her through the window. She landed in an untidy heap on the gravel courtyard below. Her left wrist bore the brunt of the impact, and she felt sharp pain radiating all the way up to her elbow.

She didn't stop to check the extent of the damage. She could see her car just feet away and jumped up, breathing heavily. She made it to the car door just as the hooded figure staggered around the side of the restroom, a hand clasped over his masked nose. She frantically pulled open the door and slid in, removing her keys from her back pocket in one smooth motion as she slammed the door closed. She peeled out of the parking lot, her whole body shaking, and swerved into the darkened main road.

Her headlights illuminated the road in front of her, and even in her state of shock and terror she could appreciate the beautiful island landscape on either side of her. The glow of the moon illuminated the waxy emerald spruce and pine needles waving in the wind. Waves in the bay sparkled like diamonds. It was a world of difference after the light pollution and urban chaos of her life in Los Angeles.

She couldn't believe she was back on Vargo Island after all these years. Finally, she had a chance to find out who had killed Carlie, to bring the memory of her best friend justice, and she was already finding herself in mortal danger. Her source had been right—this wasn't going to be easy.

She had moved away from Vargo Island—or simply

Vargo, to locals—right after graduating high school ten years ago, to study at UCLA. She was her doting parents' only child, and they had followed Maggie from Washington to LA in her junior year of college, reestablishing their veterinarian practice in the outer suburbs. She knew they missed Vargo, but their new clinic was thriving, and they all got to spend time together regularly. Though her parents had returned to Vargo for a couple of vacations, Maggie had avoided going with them. Everything about Vargo was tainted for her now. All she could think of was Carlie's death whenever she thought of her hometown.

After graduating from UCLA, she had started a career in journalism. She now worked for the *LA Times*, covering interest stories from all walks of life, but had previously been dedicated solely to the crime beat, a job that was less glamorous than its title suggested. Much of what she did was gritty and slow—long hours spent chasing down leads and convincing sources to talk to her. She spent much of her life mired in others' heartbreak, interviewing people about some of the worst moments of their lives.

Perhaps that was why it had taken her ten years to get back to Vargo. It was so painful to think of her best friend's death that being back in the town they'd grown up in, where everything reminded her of their friendship, was more than she could bear. It wasn't just Carlie's death, either. It was Maggie's memory of the last thing she'd ever said to her friend, the bitterness of the words stinging anytime she recalled them. Instead, she tried to avoid the memories, exercising some of her pain by living vicariously through others, trying to bring closure to their losses through her writing and investigations.

Only in the last couple of years, as she'd encountered corruption and cover-ups of various cases in LA, did she begin to think that perhaps something could be amiss in Carlie's death. She had never understood the ruling of drowning, since Carlie had been a champion high school swimmer, and when she'd begun to dig into the case, she had encountered roadblocks and evasiveness from the Vargo Police Department.

She had begun spending long nights hunched over her laptop, flicking through endless threads on online true crime forums, cups of coffee steaming beside her. She started crowdsourcing information online through various contacts she made, until eventually she began communicating with the anonymous source who had been sending her cryptic messages. At last, she decided that if she was ever going to get closure in Carlie's death, she needed to return to Vargo.

Suddenly, headlights flared behind her, some distance away but gaining on her. She pushed the accelerator down but knew she couldn't go too fast for fear of losing control of the car. It had been a decade since she'd driven the roads here, and at night the curves and rises were especially unfamiliar. She needed to make it to Vargo's small downtown, where she was sure there would be people. She just had to stay safe until the following morning, when she had arranged to meet her source. Then all of this would be figured out.

She navigated a curve in the road and, as she straightened out again, looked into her rearview mirror. The headlights were closer now, barely a few car lengths away. She had to keep them behind her for another few miles and she'd be on the outskirts of town and—hopefully—safe. She returned her eyes to the road and instinctively slammed on the brakes as she approached a corner too fast. She swerved desperately, trying to make the turn.

She barely had time to register what was happening before her car was spinning out of control, and everything went black.

Samuel Reyes saw a small blue sedan spin out of control in front of him, driving in the opposite direction from him, pursued closely by a sleek black pickup truck. The blue car careened wildly before slamming into the ditch on the side of the highway, diving downward so the back wheels were slightly elevated and still spinning. A thin plume of smoke rose from the hood of the destroyed vehicle.

The truck that had been pursuing so closely was now slowing down as he screeched to a halt. Samuel saw the driver was masked before they suddenly sped up and screeched away down the road. He considered pursuing it for a moment, but decided it was more important that he checked on the condition of the car crash victim.

He pulled his car to the side of the road and put on his hazard lights. Years in law enforcement put him immediately on alert. He took out the flashlight he always kept in the glove box and switched it on before walking around to the driver's side door. The door was opened, and the airbags had been deployed.

At the sound of a low groan, Samuel peered toward

the hood of the car. Someone was huddled against the front wheel, cradling their arm against their chest. As they looked up at Samuel, his heart skipped a beat.

"*Maggie?*" Samuel said incredulously.

"Sam," she responded, her voice trembling and eyes squinting against the light he was aiming at her. He lowered the flashlight and stepped toward her.

"What… I… How did this happen?" Samuel stuttered. He couldn't believe he was seeing this woman after ten years. Despite the pain pinching her face, she looked just like she had the last time he saw her, at their high school graduation. He could remember it like it was yesterday, how beautiful she had looked in her gown, freckles sprinkled across her high cheekbones and a laugh bubbling from her throat as she tossed her cap in the air.

"Long story. A little help?" Maggie asked.

"Sorry, of course." Samuel rushed over to kneel beside her. "Are you in pain?"

"My wrist. I landed on it earlier." She winced as she held it out. Samuel gently prodded the swollen skin and could already make out bruises blossoming across the area. He placed it back across her chest and signaled for her to support it with her other hand.

"Let's get you to a doctor so you can get fixed up." She turned her heart-shaped face up to look at him, her full lips pinched tight in pain. Without thinking, he reached out and wiped away a trickle of blood that had made its way down the side of Maggie's face. Instead of tenderness, Samuel felt anger blooming in his chest. A decade without seeing her, without talking to her, and this was how she was coming back into his life? Run off the road by a careless driver?

Maggie's eyes were fluttering, like she could barely keep them open. He swallowed the anger, reminding himself that Maggie was hurt and her care was the most important thing right now. "Is anyone else here?" She was whispering, her voice hoarse.

"Anyone else?" Samuel looked around in confusion. "It's just us."

"Okay," Maggie said, then closed her eyes. Samuel thought about calling an ambulance and decided it would be quicker to drive her to the tiny medical center in downtown Vargo, maybe ten minutes away. There was a strong likelihood it would still be open, and it would take much longer for an air ambulance to arrive from the mainland.

"I'm going to get you to a doctor," Samuel told her.

"Someone tried to attack me at the public rest area back there. I'm pretty sure they were tailing my car just now. They ran me off the road," Maggie murmured.

Samuel thought back to the car that had sped away as he pulled up to the crash. "I did see a car, but it raced off when I got here." He absorbed what Maggie had just said. "Someone attacked you?"

"That's how I injured my wrist—trying to escape." Maggie's face was drained of color. Her lips were a deep scarlet against her blanched skin.

"Maggie, I need you to try and stay awake. You might have a concussion." Samuel shook her shoulder gently. He decided to put the conversation about the attacker on the back burner for now. Her health was the more pressing need.

"I'm awake." Maggie opened her eyes and looked at him. A deep ultramarine like the ocean, just as he remembered. He would gaze surreptitiously at her for the entire block of their senior English class, just to get a glimpse of those eyes.

"Good. Let's get to my truck and we'll head straight to the doctors." He helped her up and kept an arm around her as they walked to his pickup truck. He opened the passenger door and helped her to clamber in, buckling her seat belt so she didn't have to use her injured arm. "I'm going to call a contact of mine on the local force to come and take a look at the wreck and get your car sorted."

"Police?" Maggie sounded wary.

"Yeah, an officer named Joey Bartlett. He helped a friend of mine out when their house was robbed." Samuel studied Maggie as she bit her lip, obviously going back and forth about agreeing. He wondered what could be making her unsure about calling the police. Was she in some sort of trouble? Was her crash related to that?

"Okay," Maggie relented finally. "But I'm not talking to any police tonight."

"Maggie, is everything okay? Are you in some kind of trouble? You can tell me," Samuel asked gently. Maggie shook her head but didn't speak. He could tell she wasn't going to share anything else right now.

Samuel shut her door and called Joey; explaining the situation. Joey agreed to take care of the car and meet Samuel at the hospital the next morning. Vargo had a tiny force that served all of the local islands. He was grateful it wasn't a busy night and Joey was actually available. After hanging up, Samuel grabbed some flashing disc lights he kept in his emergency kit. He laid them out on the road so no other cars would hit the wreck and jumped into his truck.

As he turned the truck around and began heading back into town, he tried to get her talking again. "You said you wouldn't talk to any police. Are you in legal trouble?"

"No," Maggie laughed. "I haven't committed any crimes. I think someone is unhappy about a project I'm working on."

"A project?" Samuel probed.

"I'm a journalist. I think someone is trying to shut me up." Her words had a tone of finality, and he got the distinct sense she didn't want to talk anymore. He'd known she was a journalist, and had followed her career for a while, looking for her pieces in the *LA Times*. A few years ago, he'd made the decision to stop reading her articles and accept that their friendship was over. He needed to move on.

Now, she had landed back in his life in the most chaotic way possible.

"You know, Maggie, you said you wouldn't talk to the police—but I'm in law enforcement. At least, I was." Samuel looked at her briefly before turning back to face the road. He could feel Maggie's gaze on him.

"FBI, right?" she asked.

"How did you know?"

"Like I said, I'm a journalist. I have my ways of keeping track of people." Maggie laughed again, but Samuel felt no good humor. His chest tightened with bitterness. She could keep track of him anonymously, from a distance, but she couldn't return any of the calls or emails he'd written to her in the years after she'd left Vargo?

Silence froze the air between them. Maggie was correct—he was an FBI agent. He had also left Vargo Island after high school, only returning after a set of traumatic events left him needing space and rest. Ever since, he had felt adrift, looking for anything he could cling to for balance.

Just over a year ago, he had been shot while working a case for the FBI as a criminal profiler. It had been his dream job, one he'd been working toward since graduating college. He rose through the ranks quickly, and he was working a murder case as a profiler when he and his partner were pinned down under gunfire. His partner was killed at the scene, and Samuel was shot three times. One bullet did minor damage, grazing his shoulder, but the other two struck him in his right thigh, causing permanent nerve damage.

After taking a few weeks of medical leave, his supervisor put him on administrative duty, since his injury precluded him from working in the field. His new role sucked the life from him. He'd always been a man of action, and paperwork had never been his passion or his strong suit. After a couple of months, he requested extended leave from the Bureau to try and figure out his future, which was granted. His supervisor promised to hold his job for a year. That was nine months ago, and Samuel still wasn't sure what he was going to do.

He could feel the pain from the bullet damage in his

thigh even now and rubbed the spot around his quadricep that felt as if it were contracting so tightly and painfully it might snap. He looked over to Maggie and noticed her eyes were still drooping. His bitterness was replaced with concern, and he sighed.

As he drove down the highway he tried to keep her awake. “Maggie, what’s going on? Can you just tell me why you’re back?”

“Like I said, it’s a long story.” Maggie groaned as she readjusted in the seat. “It’s cold, do you mind if I turn up the heat?”

“I think that will make you sleepier. It’s just a few minutes more to the hospital. Let’s keep it cool so you don’t fall asleep,” Samuel suggested.

“Eternally practical.” Maggie grinned. They made brief eye contact. So many years since he’d seen her, and it was jarring to find the connection between them was still just as strong. He thought about their senior year of high school, Maggie cheering him on in the stands during football games, him catching all of her soccer games. They were such good friends to each other, though he always harbored a desire for more than friendship—not that he’d ever told her.

“Tell me the reason you’re really here. You know you can trust me,” Samuel said quietly. He knew when she was being evasive, and he certainly wasn’t getting the whole truth. She had always been stubbornly independent, but he wanted to help.

“It’s about Carlie,” Maggie said after a pause. The name sat between them like a boulder, heavy and dangerous. He saw her reach up to her neck and clasp a small golden necklace. "I never stopped trying to find out what happened."

The death of Maggie's best friend, Carlie, had changed their lives. Maggie and Samuel had become close in their last couple of years of high school, but she had been best friends with Carlie since elementary school. They were a common sight, walking the halls of the school, Carlie's tall, bronzed limbs contrasting against Maggie's petite porcelain figure.

"I thought Carlie drowned?" Samuel said. That was the official explanation, but rumors that Carlie had actually been murdered continued to swirl among locals. Even now he still occasionally heard people discussing the case with suspicion. He had never given the rumors much credence. In fact, any time he heard Carlie brought up he avoided the conversation. It made him think of Maggie, and what they had lost.

"That's what the police said, but I'm sure they know there's major irregularities. I'm fighting to get it reopened." Maggie's angry tone told Samuel she hadn't been successful so far. "I've been researching her death lately. I've been trawling message boards and true crime groups online, trying to find out more information. Her death has so many…inconsistencies. I figure *someone* has to know *something*."

That senior year, just months before graduation, Carlie's body had been found on the beach of South Rock Island, a small island off the coast of Vargo. It was steep and overgrown, with only a tiny sliver of rocky beach on one side, so it was never a popular tourist destination. The only locals that frequented it were hunters and some avid outdoor enthusiasts. There was also a maze of underground tunnels that some visited for spelunking.

Carlie had been found on the frigid South Rock beach in February, when it was still cold and the weather was unpredictable. The police ruled it a drowning but never elaborated on why they thought she was found there alone in the winter.

Rumors and whispers heightened the whole situation. Carlie had been a straight A student, but in her senior year she began dating Shepherd Todd, the son of a high-ranking local politician who was now a governor in a different state. Shep was known to be wild, a possible drug dealer—and certainly user—who was constantly protected by his father. It was Shep who reported Carlie's death. He claimed she'd left him a note saying she was going on an adventure to the island and wanted him to meet her there after school, and he found her dead body on the beach when he went looking for her.

"You think someone killed Carlie?" Samuel asked.

"Maybe. It's been hard to find definitive information," Maggie said.

"What made you want to start looking into Carlie's death more?"

"For years I kept her at the back of my mind. It was too painful to go there," Maggie admitted quietly, tugging unconsciously at her necklace. "But I'm a journalist now, and after spending a few years investigating the deaths and losses of other people, I realized I needed to confront what happened to Carlie." She took a deep breath, biting her lower lip. "I'm really blessed, actually. My editor, Everett, is amazing. She's a talented techie and an incredible writer, and she gives me a lot of latitude to work on interesting pieces. When I explained I was investigating Carlie's death, it was actually Everett who suggested I write a long-form article about it and gave me all the resources I needed to explore." Maggie yawned widely as Samuel slowed down and pulled into the medical center parking lot.

"Let's not think about this anymore tonight. C'mon, I'll bring you in." Samuel put his truck in Park and turned off the ignition. "I think I know who the doctor on call tonight is."

He got out and came to assist Maggie out of the truck. As he helped her step down, he saw a truck driving slowly down the road in front of the medical center. He studied it carefully, realizing it was the same truck that had been driving behind Maggie when she crashed. He began to run toward it, hoping to get a glimpse of the license plate.

He had barely taken a few steps when the driver gunned it down the road, peeling out on the asphalt in a cloud of thick exhaust fumes before he could make out any identifying details of either the truck or the driver. Samuel knew instinctively that Maggie was right—someone had intentionally run her off the road. Whatever she was mixed up in, she was in danger. He was beginning to suspect that someone didn't want her to uncover the truth of Carlie's death.

TWO

It was after midnight, and Maggie was utterly exhausted. True to his word, Samuel had known the doctor on call. In fact, Maggie had known her, too. Jennifer Simms had gone to their high school and graduated a couple of years before them. She'd come back to work at the small medical practice in downtown Vargo. Even *small* was stretching the truth—it was a tiny doctor's office that was chronically understaffed.

Dr. Simms had given her a thorough examination. Maggie had a sprained wrist and some lacerations and contusions but otherwise would be fine. They put her wrist in a brace and secured it to her chest in a sling to rest it. At Dr. Simms's strong recommendation, Maggie had agreed to stay overnight for observation in case of a concussion, but she could be discharged in time to make her morning meeting if she was doing well.

"I'll have our overnight nurse continue to monitor you through the night. My shift is finishing shortly," Dr. Simms said, accompanying Maggie from the examination room into a small room with a neatly made bed. They both stopped in their tracks at seeing Samuel sitting in a chair by the window. Maggie hadn't expected him to still be here—though she had to admit, she had hoped he might stay.

Maggie quickly tightened her hospital gown around her and let the doctor help her into the bed. Samuel walked over to them.

"Thanks, Jen," he said softly, smiling at Dr. Simms and touching her elbow gently. She nodded in response and quickly left the room. Maggie watched her go, wondering what kind of relationship she had with Samuel. They were obviously very familiar with each other. Maggie shook her head to clear the thoughts away. She hadn't seen the man in over a decade and there was no point revisiting old feelings now. She lifted her hand to her neck and panicked suddenly as she felt only skin, but quickly remembered she'd taken her necklace off for her examination. It was in the clear hospital bag on her bedside table, sitting with her phone and wallet. She pulled the necklace out of the bag and clasped it back around her neck. It was half of a friendship necklace, one she'd been given for her fifteenth birthday.

"How are you feeling?" Samuel asked. Maggie tilted her face toward him and felt bathed in a warm light of safety by his presence. He was just like she remembered, though he now sported some tawny bristles along his square jaw and a few more lines joined the dimples radiating from his smile. Otherwise, he could have stepped out of her memory from the last time she saw him all those years ago. Her stomach tightened as he rested his large hand on her shoulder for a moment, before stepping back with his hands in his pockets.

She smiled. "I'm fine. Dr. Simms says I can be discharged tomorrow so I'll still be able to make my meeting."

"Meeting?" Confusion surged in his amber eyes.

"Yeah, it's kind of a big reason I'm back." Maggie suddenly felt guilty, like she'd been keeping a secret from Samuel. "I have a source that claims to have information about Carlie's death, but they told me not to talk to anyone, especially the police."

"Who is the source?" Samuel's voice was concerned. "Do you know them?"

"They contacted me through an online message board." Maggie's explanation sounded far-fetched, even to her. For a moment she wondered if she was completely insane for doing this, for trusting this random online contact and leaving her life behind in LA for what could be a wild-goose chase. "They had posted pretty regularly on a discussion board thread I created about Carlie's death, and they seemed to know a lot. They want to meet somewhere local. I'm waiting to hear where they suggest."

"I can't believe you are going to meet some stranger from the internet alone." Samuel's jaw was set tightly, and Maggie knew he was upset. "What if this 'contact' is the same person who attacked you earlier? And if they really had information, why do they need to meet you in person? They could just as easily reveal what they have in email or over the phone."

"I assume it's because they have evidence to show me," Maggie said quietly. She had been researching Carlie's death for years, and this source was the closest she'd come to actually getting any real information. She had to believe they were legitimate, or she might never find out what had happened to her best friend. She could feel tears seeping from the corners of her eyes, and she wiped them away impatiently.

"I'm just worried about you." Samuel's face had softened, and he grasped her free hand. The skin on his fingers was slightly rough, as though it belonged to someone who worked with their hands. Maggie had tried to keep Samuel from her mind over the years, but now and then she'd checked in on him, using her talents to find out that he'd studied forensics in college and joined the FBI. Other than that, she knew very little about his life now, and felt selfish for not asking more. "I think you should consider reporting the attack to the police. I have a good friend who works with the local force. I know you could trust him."

"I can't." Maggie was torn, though. She normally wouldn't hesitate in reporting something like this to the police, but she also didn't want to jeopardize her investigative work. Besides, after Carlie's death had been ruled an accidental drowning and the police refused to reopen the case or discuss it further with her, Maggie had no trust in them.

Samuel sighed and rubbed his eyes tiredly. His gaze landed on her necklace. She was absentmindedly twisting the half heart on its chain, a nervous habit she'd developed. "I remember you wearing that necklace in high school." Samuel motioned to her hand.

"Carlie gave it to me for my fifteenth birthday. I almost never take it off. It's my physical reminder of what she meant to me." Maggie rubbed her finger along the jagged edge, felt the letters *B-E* and *F-R-I* engraved on one side. She dug out a photo from her wallet and showed it to Samuel. It was a photo of Carlie. "Her dad gave me this photo. It was taken the day she was killed. It reminds me every day that Carlie lost her life somehow, and I'm going to find out why. That's why I'm still meeting the source tomorrow."

Maggie knew the photo like the back of her hand. It was a selfie Carlie had taken the morning she died, in the front garden of her house. Framed by a beautiful flowering ocean spray shrub, Carlie's stunning almond eyes stared up at the camera, a coy smile curving her full lips. It cut off below her shoulders, but Maggie knew from other eyewitness accounts of that day that Carlie had been wearing a galaxy-printed crew neck sweatshirt and acid-washed jeans.

Samuel stared at the photo for a long moment before handing it back to Maggie with a sad nod. "It's a beautiful photo of her."

"It's how I like to remember her," Maggie whispered, tucking the photo back in her wallet. She didn't mention the other memory that she tried to keep pushed down, the memory that was driving her insistence in investigating this case. It was the memory of the last interaction she'd ever had with Carlie.

The last day they'd spoken, she and Carlie had had a huge fight. They'd bickered before, but nothing serious. They'd had plans to go and see a movie on the mainland, an activity they loved doing together. They'd pair the movie with a little shopping and some greasy fast food for lunch—all the things they really couldn't do on Vargo. Maggie had waited at the ferry terminal for Carlie, just as they'd planned, but the ferry left without Carlie arriving, leaving Maggie impatiently watching it depart from the Vargo shore.

She'd rushed over to Carlie's house, worried something had happened to her, only to find her friend leaving the house herself, hand in hand with her boyfriend, Shep. They looked like catalog models—perfectly groomed with big easy smiles, though Carlie's smile faded when she'd seen the thunderous look on Maggie's face.

Her best friend had totally forgotten about their plans, so enamored was she with Shep. It had infuriated Maggie, and as Carlie tried to apologize and explain that she'd forgotten about going to the movie, that Shep had planned a date for them, Maggie had exploded. The last thing Maggie had yelled at Carlie was that she was being a fool and that she and Shep deserved each other, before turning on her heel and rushing home without looking back.

Maggie closed her eyes against the painful memory. Her heart filled with regret every time she thought of that last interaction. Even as she'd walked away, she knew she had overreacted. She was just so tired of being blown off for Carlie's dates with Shep, so tired of watching her friend put Shep ahead of everything in her life—ahead of her family, school, sports, and friends.

"It's late." Samuel sighed resignedly. "How about you get some sleep, and tomorrow I'll take you to meet this source of yours."

"No, I have to go alone," Maggie said firmly. She tucked the photo back in her wallet.

"And how are you going to get there? We left your car in a ditch, remember?" Samuel paused, and Maggie couldn't think of a response. Samuel smiled in triumph. Maggie's heart skipped a beat at the familiar way one corner of his lips rose up higher than the other, making his smile adorably lopsided. "I'll sleep in this chair, and we'll head out tomorrow morning. I'll even wait out of sight, if you insist."

"Fine. But don't sleep here. It's not necessary. Do you live far?" Maggie was touched by his offer to stay, but she always worked alone. After years of chasing down stories she had become used to getting things done by herself. It was easier. She didn't have to rely on anyone, and she didn't have to be disappointed.

"I'm staying at my grandfather's cabin, the one down at the bay. It's about ten minutes from here." Samuel motioned back the way they'd driven from. "I was heading home from meeting some friends in town when I came across you, actually."

Maggie could remember the cabin. She had spent a lot of time with Samuel there, sunbathing and kayaking and swimming. It was hard to recall the feeling of safety she'd always had there, as she felt her life in mortal danger now. Fear burned like acid in her stomach, churning like a storm. She swallowed the nausea down and said, "Go home and get some sleep. If you insist on bringing me, be back here early."

"Yes, ma'am," Samuel responded wryly. He squeezed her hand one last time, and she watched his broad shoulders as he turned and left the room. She collapsed back against the cool hospital pillows, exhaustion fighting against the adrenaline that hummed in her body.

She couldn't believe that even after all these years, her fondness for Samuel could sneak back in so easily. She visualized a large vault, and imagined her feelings being locked back in that vault. She needed to remain on her guard, she couldn't risk any kind of distraction. So many things had changed since high school. There was no point rehashing old feelings. It would only lead to heartache.

She had dated sporadically while living in LA but she had never met anyone she really connected with there. In truth, her life was consumed with her career. She considered it her life's mission to bring the truth to light for those who didn't have a voice, and that was more than a full-time job. A small voice inside her questioned whether it was really about work, or whether she was scared of being hurt, knowing firsthand how tenuous life can be—but Maggie pushed the thoughts aside.

The nurse came in to check her vitals and then she must have drifted off, because when she next opened her eyes, the digital clock next to her bed read 5:08 a.m. She blinked confusedly, wondering what had woken her. A figure was silhouetted against the moonlight streaming in through the window. *The nurse again*, Maggie thought groggily, pushing herself into a sitting position.

The figure lurched toward her, taking her by surprise. She opened her mouth to scream and raised her free hand, but the attacker swatted her hand aside like it was an annoying fly. He pinned her on the bed, his fingers clamping tightly around her throat and squeezing with tremendous force. As he leaned his considerable weight on her, her throat closed and she was unable to make a sound. Adrenaline sent waves of panic coursing through her. She tried to push against him but he was too strong.

Lord, I need You! Maggie managed a silent prayer as her vision began to swim. Her lungs were in agony, and her throat burned. She knew this was the same person who'd attacked her at the public restrooms—he had the same black gaiter mask and hooded sweatshirt, the same blue eyes that flashed like glaciers in the moonlight. She tried to sort through her memories of a self-defense class taken years ago. Suddenly, a word rang out like a clarion bell in her mind. *Eyes!*

Using her good hand, she deftly dug a thumb into his eyes, sinking into the socket deeply. He let out a muffled grunt but his grasp didn't let up. Darkness was edging in at the corners of her vision, and she knew she was losing consciousness. *This is it. I'm going to die*. Maggie's thoughts were racing, terrified. *Lord, it can't end like this. Deliver me from danger.*

"What is going on here?" The words spoken from the doorway were quickly followed by a scream for help as her attacker let go and spun around. The sudden rush of oxygen left Maggie gasping air like a fish out of water, and she slipped off the edge of her bed and onto the floor. The masked man ran from the room, pushing past the nurse who had interrupted him and causing her to stagger backward into her medical cart.

"H-help," Maggie managed to sputter. She was in shock. Someone had just tried to kill her…again. A chasm of darkness swam at the edge of her vision, and as she slumped to the floor, the world faded to black.

It was still dark outside, the heavy black silk of the sky pressing against the horizon, as Samuel began his routine. He sat on his porch, as was his morning custom, nursing a mug of black coffee and letting the natural splendors surrounding him lighten his soul. His grandfather's cabin was small but well-appointed, largely due to the time, money and energy Samuel had invested in remodeling it since he moved in. The porch afforded a stunning view out into the bay, and it connected with a long series of steps that led to a small boat launch.

Samuel took a sip of coffee and thought about Maggie. He had packed a bag with some fresh clothes, deodorant and a bottle of water for her, since they'd forgotten her suitcase in the trunk of the wrecked car. The backpack was sitting in his truck, ready to go to the medical center. He felt a little uneasy about offering her the clothes. They had belonged to his ex-girlfriend, who also happened to be the doctor treating Maggie, Jennifer Simms. When he'd been digging through his clothes, trying to find something that would fit Maggie's diminutive frame, he found an old hoodie and pair of sweatpants that Jennifer had used when she helped him paint the cabin. He must have offered to wash them and forgotten about them. Both items of clothing still had paint stains, but at least they would fit Maggie comfortably.

He stood up to lean against the railing of his balcony, pouring the dregs of his coffee over the side. His leg ached, and he stretched it, massaging the tight knot of pain. He'd been through three separate surgeries to fix the majority of the damage, but he knew he would have to manage the pain for the rest of his life. He was blessed to be left with only a slight limp.

He lifted his face to the rising sun, pastel hues of red and yellow painting the water beneath him. Even with his life in a state of confusion, he was grateful every day for the bounty of living here. A few weeks before he took his extended leave, his mother broke the news that his grandfather had died, leaving the cabin to Samuel in his will. Samuel was an only child, raised by a single mom who now lived in Seattle but had raised him in Vargo. Samuel had been very close to his grandfather, who was really like a father to him. His death had been the final momentum Samuel needed to take a leave of absence from the Bureau.

He sublet his apartment in Bellingham and moved out to the cabin. The pain from his leg made it difficult to sleep, and when he managed to sleep he had nightmares, so he spent a lot of nights completely gutting and remodeling the cabin. During the day he would kayak, trying to maintain his upper body strength, and pushed himself to run and hike longer and more challenging trails to rebuild the strength in his leg.

Samuel had met Jennifer Simms when he first moved back to Vargo. They had briefly dated, and their relationship ended amicably when they realized they were better off as friends. The experience made Samuel realize how consumed he was with guilt over his partner's death, and he knew he wasn't in any sort of headspace to pursue a romantic relationship.

Samuel wondered if there was something wrong with *him*. He had left a job he had worked years for, and broken up with a wonderful woman, because things didn't *feel right*. The guilt he felt about surviving the shooting while his partner died chewed him up. He worried that nothing would ever feel right again. Knowing his leave of absence would be over in a matter of months filled him with unease. He found he wasn't excited about the thought of returning to what had once been his dream job. His hopes and priorities had shifted with his injury and the death of his partner. Looking into the future was like gazing through an unfocused camera lens, whereas before it had always been clear.

His cell phone rang, breaking his reverie. He pulled it from his pocket. "Hello?"

"Samuel? It's Jennifer."

"Jennifer? What's going on? Is Maggie okay?" Samuel was already walking toward his truck, moving unconsciously.

"Look, she's going to be okay…but someone just attacked her in her hospital room. Our security guard has been talking to her, but she doesn't want to call the police. I think you should come in." Jennifer's words were brief but concerned.

"I'm on my way." Samuel hung up without saying goodbye, grabbed his keys and got straight into his truck. He tore off down the bumpy gravel driveway that connected the cabin to the larger paved road that laced the cliffs, then raced toward the hospital. As he drove he called Joey Bartlett, his contact on the force. He was really a friend of a friend, and even though Maggie seemed to have a deep distrust of the local police, Samuel needed to call on a law enforcement contact.

"Hi, Samuel," Joey said, picking up after a couple of rings.

"I need a favor," Samuel said, skipping the small talk. "Can you meet me at the medical center in ten minutes?"

"Of course." Joey didn't ask any other questions, reaffirming to Samuel why he had chosen to call him. He sped the whole way to the doctor's, hoping no cops were on traffic duty. He kept uttering the same prayer over and over. *Dear Lord, keep her safe.* As he prayed, he felt a warmth in his chest. He realized part of why he'd been feeling so lost was that he hadn't been turning to God for years. It was like confiding in a familiar friend after a long absence.

He parked near the main doors and nearly broke the land speed record running to her room, the backpack looped over his shoulder. A security guard was posted outside her door, and he held up his hand to tell Samuel to stop before the door opened and Jennifer ushered Samuel in.

Samuel breathed a sigh of relief to see Maggie sitting up in bed, sipping water, but the relief quickly dissipated. Violet bruises had spread around her throat, giving her neck the hue of angry storm clouds. Her face was drained, just like last night. She put her water down and smiled at Samuel as he walked in, then lay back against the pillows. He couldn't help thinking she looked like a Renaissance painting, the window casting a single source of warm light on her contemplative expression, her auburn curls framing her face.

"Samuel, hey." Joey walked in behind him, accompanied by another officer.

"Hi, Joey. Thanks for this." Samuel shook Joey's hand in greeting, then turned to Maggie. "I am so sorry this happened to you, Maggie. This is my police contact, Joey. You are obviously being targeted and we need to put some things in place to keep you safe."

"Okay," Maggie relented, her voice raspy. Samuel could see there was an internal struggle, and he realized she was still prioritizing her investigation before her own safety. She had always been doggedly determined, and it was obvious that determination had only increased over the years. "But we have to leave soon."

"You still want to go?" Samuel was shocked.

"Of course. This changes nothing." Maggie turned to look at Joey, a bemused expression on his face. "I can give you ten minutes."

"That should be fine. My colleague here is going to take some pictures of your injuries and collect some samples from under your fingernails. I'll ask you a few questions." Joey nodded at Samuel.

"I'll wait outside," Samuel said to Maggie, who also nodded. He placed the backpack on the end of Maggie's bed before leaving the room.

Outside the hospital room, Jennifer paused next to Samuel.

"It's a blast from the past—seeing Maggie Dalton," she said in a studiously casual voice. "You always did have a soft spot for her."

"Yeah, well…it was a long time ago," said Samuel gruffly. Jennifer raised her eyebrows in a manner that showed she didn't believe him, before the exhausted night nurse waved her over, medical charts spilling from her arms. She began to walk away.

"Jennifer?"

She turned back to look at him.

"Thank you. For helping her, and for calling me," Samuel said sincerely. Jennifer nodded and strode off.

Samuel walked a few paces to the end of the hallway, looking out the window that overlooked the parking lot and the road they'd traveled the night before. The weight of the situation sat heavily on his shoulders. Maggie—of all people—was in danger, and he couldn't figure out why. His mind raced through the possibilities. Was this related to something from her career as a journalist? There were so many stories and so many people that she could have angered along the way. He thought back to the headlines he'd seen over the years, the high-profile cases she'd covered, the power players she had exposed. Could it be an old grudge from one of them?

Or could this really be related to her investigation into Carlie's death? The more he thought about it, the more he had to admit it was a possibility—someone didn't want her digging into things that were meant to stay buried. Either way, he knew one thing for sure: Whatever was going on, he couldn't stand by and let it happen. He had to figure it out if he wanted to keep her safe.

Moments later, the door to Maggie's room opened and Joey waved him in. The other officer had just finished photographing her neck and was packing the camera back into its small bag.

"We've got Maggie's statement and some fingernail

samples and photos. We'll do our best now to figure out who did this," Joey said, tucking a small notebook and pencil into the front pocket of his shirt.

"I wasn't much assistance. I couldn't really see the guy's face or anything, just his eyes." Maggie shrugged.

"Every little bit helps," Joey said. He looked over at Samuel. "She wouldn't tell me where she's headed to for this meeting, but someone is obviously determined to harm her. I think it would be best if you accompany her."

"I plan to." Samuel was firm. Joey nodded. They exchanged goodbyes, and as soon as Joey left, Maggie sat up in bed and swung her legs out from under the blanket.

"Let's get going," she said. Samuel sensed nerves bubbling underneath her cool exterior, but didn't push it.

"Are you planning on island hopping wearing a hospital gown?" he asked.

"If I have to," Maggie responded, her chin raised obstinately. Samuel burst out laughing.

"Check the backpack. There's a change of clothes in there. I'll be outside when you're done."

He went to leave and saw Maggie's hands trembling as she reached for the backpack. He paused, turning back to her. "Maggie, do you want to talk about what happened?"

"I've told you everything I know," she said shortly.

"This would all be a lot easier if you let me in," Samuel said, surprising himself at his forthrightness. Samuel was a man of few words outside the office, his quiet demeanor often mistaken for detachment. At work it was different—he was decisive, his every move deliberate and authoritative. In the field, his forthrightness commanded respect, but in personal matters, he retreated behind a wall of silence, unwilling to let anyone see past the hard exterior he had built over years of keeping his emotions in check.

"I can do this by myself," Maggie insisted, though he thought she seemed a little less sure of herself than earlier. "I'm not going to let someone bully me into stopping my investigation."

"You were strangled, Maggie. Someone is trying to *kill* you. I think this goes a bit further than bullying." Samuel's hands were in his pockets, fists clenched in fury at whoever had attacked Maggie.

"It doesn't change anything," Maggie said, her mouth forming a stubborn line. Samuel wondered if she was trying to convince herself, as well as him. "Someone is willing to attack me because I'm investigating Carlie's death. Can't you see what that means?"

"Yeah." Samuel nodded slowly. "It means someone wants to keep you quiet because you're onto something." He paused for a moment, then met her eyes. "It also means your life is in mortal danger."

THREE

Maggie read the text again for what felt like the hundredth time.

Boat house on South Rock Island. 9:00 am.

The message had arrived this morning as she was getting changed in her hospital room. Samuel had brought her a pair of gray sweatpants and a gray zip-up hoodie. The clothes were slightly too big and splattered with old paint, but comfortable. When she'd put her hands inside the hoodie pockets, she'd found an old library card, the name printed on it reading *Jennifer Simms*. She recognized it as the name of her doctor, whom Samuel had seemed familiar with last night.

They're dating, Maggie thought to herself. Her emotions felt muddied, like trying to see the bottom of a pool of brackish water. It was a shock, having Samuel return to her life in such a chaotic way after years of keeping anything to do with him locked away in an emotional vault. There were conflicting feelings swirling within her, seeing the life he'd built for himself here, in a place that felt so damaged to her now. Ultimately, the fear and shock she was experiencing at the events of the last twelve hours held her attention the most.

She looked over at Samuel, who had most likely saved her life. He had been the captain of the high school football team and a popular honor roll student. Maggie was a talented soccer player but much quieter and with a small circle of friends. She couldn't really pinpoint when she and Samuel had become friends. Their connection was unexpected. At first, Maggie had been sure he was feigning interest in spending time with her. She'd assumed he was just another dumb jock who wanted to copy her notes in class, until she realized he was just as academically advanced as she was. She had begun to trust him, and soon they were spending more and more time together, their friend groups overlapping. She fell in love with him quickly, but was never brave enough to tell him her true feelings.

She looked over at Samuel as he drove, but quickly turned back to the window. She wasn't in the right mind frame to wander back down this particular memory lane. Samuel had been silent much of the car ride, and by the tightness of his jaw Maggie could tell he wasn't happy about her choice to go ahead with meeting the source.

"I can't believe we'll be going to the place Carlie was killed," Maggie said, breaking the tense silence. The meeting location had surprised her, but she chalked it up to the source wanting to show her something about the crime scene. That would explain why their meeting couldn't just happen virtually. Samuel merely raised his eyebrows in a studiously neutral response, but Maggie could see his jaw clench even more, a muscle ticking in its defined lines.

She looked out the window again and turned her phone over and over in her hand, thinking about the photograph on it that was the only other solid piece of evidence in her investigation. It was a photo she'd snapped of the coroner's report issued for Carlie's death, a copy of which she had managed to get from Carlie's grandfather when she'd visited them a while ago. A knot tightened in her stomach as she thought about it. The sterile, cold words felt almost surreal against the memory of her best friend's laughter; the facts listed on the page didn't line up against the girl Carlie had been.

She wondered whether she should tell Samuel. She hadn't told anyone about it except her editor. Over many years, she had learned to guard her sources and evidence closely. She trusted Samuel, and yet this was the first time she'd seen him in ten years. She wasn't ready to share everything she had.

Instead, she asked, "Do you know the area? This boathouse?" She was jiggling her knees and twisting her hair around her finger, habits born out of nerves, while anxiety sloshed leadenly in the pit of her stomach. She and Samuel had eaten bagels from the café next to the doctor's, and now she was worried she might bring the food back up. She took deep breaths through her nose to try and quell her nausea.

"Yeah, I do. South Rock is only accessible by boat. It's off the tourist trails because it doesn't have a lot of beach spots or hiking trails. It's totally uninhabited apart from a couple of hunting cabins." Samuel checked his mirrors and signaled to turn onto a small winding road.

"I know a few guys who like to go out there hunting, and my grandpa took me hunting there once. You can also get into the Labyrinth Caves at low tide. I've actually been there before with a friend, but spelunking is not really my scene. Too much risk, too little reward."

The caves were popular among thrill-seekers and some local teenagers. They could be dangerous at high tide, and Maggie knew of at least one person who had been killed while exploring the cave system.

They drove in silence awhile longer. Samuel had offered to use his motorboat to take Maggie out to the island, and she had reluctantly agreed. She could rent a kayak, but she knew her arm would severely limit her paddling power. Besides, it had been so long since she'd navigated the waters. On a calm day it was delightful, but the tides were savage and she didn't want to get caught out.

Maggie surveyed the early spring day around her. Trees were beginning to awaken from their winter slumber, delicate buds unfurling on skeletal branches. The gunmetal gray rocks that hugged the rugged coastline sported patches of vibrant moss. She could even see the chiffony heads of a few wildflowers nodding in patches of grass. Seeing the natural beauty around her was bittersweet, bringing up her happiest memories as well as her most painful.

As the scenery unfurled through her window, a prayer rang through her mind, unprompted. *Thank You, Lord. Thank You for the happy memories, and thank You for what I've learned from the hard times. Thank You for giving me the chance to honor Carlie's memory. Help me to bring those who harmed her to justice.* She breathed deeply as she prayed, feeling her stomach settling. She raised her hand and twisted the half heart that lay below her throat. Her thumb traced a familiar path over the name carved into the back—*CARLIE*. On the other half, which Carlie had always worn, it said *MAGGIE*.

Samuel stopped his truck in the driveway of his small cabin. It was different from what Maggie remembered. Whereas before it had been a little run down, she could see it had recently had a lot of work poured into it. The outside shone with a fresh coat of bright white paint, the shutters and front door a matte black. A low picket fence had been erected, with sage and northern sea oats planted carefully around its edges.

"The cabin looks beautiful," Maggie commented.

"Thanks," Samuel responded distractedly. He was looking at his phone, eyebrows knitted together in concern.

"Is cvcrything okay?" Maggic askcd aftcr a pausc. Samuel looked up.

"Just got a weather alert. There's a storm blowing in."

"Is it serious?"

"Looks like it. Ferry services to Vargo are going to be suspended until at least early evening." Samuel frowned. "Heavy rain and winds, dangerous ocean conditions."

"That doesn't bode well." Maggie crossed her arms and looked out across the bay. The sky shimmered an innocent periwinkle blue, but she knew that storms blew in fast here, like freight trains barreling down the tracks—silent at first, then suddenly roaring to life, tearing through everything in its path before fading away just as quickly.

"Are you still sure this is something you need to do?" Samuel asked.

"Yes." Maggie was firm. "I don't expect you to risk your safety, though."

"Mags, c'mon. I've got your back," Samuel said. That simple sentence rocked her carefully constructed defenses. That had been the shared mantra they'd repeat to each other before sporting events or tests. She remembered her nerves before the state semifinal soccer game in her senior year. Samuel had hugged her and whispered, "You've got this, Mags, and I've got your back."

"You always have," Maggie replied.

"I think if we leave the island before eleven, we should be okay," Samuel said, though he sounded concerned. He dug through a case in the back of his truck and pulled out two pairs of navy gaiters. He threw a pair to Maggie and began pulling the other on. "These will help keep our pants dry."

"I don't have a jacket," Maggie said as she pulled the gaiters on. Samuel dug around in the case again.

"This should do the job." He offered Maggie a plastic rain poncho. Despite the clear skies, she pulled it on over her clothes, knowing she'd probably get dampened on the boat ride. Samuel zipped up his own rain jacket.

"Thanks for all of this," Maggie said sincerely. Samuel nodded with a lopsided, nonchalant smile. It was an endearing quirk that she once loved, but that Samuel had always been a little self-conscious about. He led the way down the steep set of stairs in front of the house.

At the bottom, tied to a tiny jetty, Samuel's old motorboat bobbed in the water. It was a simple boat, its white paint wearing off in patches, with a small outboard motor mounted on the back.

He held out a hand and helped her in, then untied the boat and turned on the small engine. It came to life with a throaty roar, and Samuel steered them out into the inlet. In less than fifteen minutes they were approaching the island, its sheer sides rising from the waters. Samuel cut the engine and they glided toward the tiny half-moon bay, smooth rocks glittering above the tide line.

The island's visage reminded Maggie of a hidden gem, cradled by mist and towering evergreen trees, its rugged shores untouched by time and offering solitude in the embrace of the sea. For all its beauty, a palpable sense of unease hung in the air, as though the island itself was holding its breath. The silence was heavy, broken only by the soft lapping of waves against jagged rocks. The wildness of the place, untouched and untamed, felt like a warning, as if the island were guarding a secret. Maggie could feel the hairs on her arms bristling in alarm.

A steep hill rose up above the beach. The only access through the overgrown grass was a narrow dirt path that threaded through it. Tucked up against the base of the hill stood a dilapidated boathouse, the weather-beaten structure old and worn. Rocks crunched as Samuel dragged the boat up onto the shore. Maggie took his hand and jumped out. Pulled up against the opposite end of the shore was a tiny boat with a similar outboard motor to the one Samuel had.

"There's someone here," Maggie noted, craning her

neck to try and see if someone was on the hill above them. "Hello?" Maggie called loudly. She checked her phone again to see if someone had texted her, but there was nothing.

"Maybe it's a hunter?" Samuel said, though he sounded unsure.

"Maybe," Maggie agreed, similar trepidation rising in her voice. She took a moment to take in the enormity of what she was looking at. This was where Carlie's body had been found by Shep all those years ago. She still remembered her parents sitting her down to tell her the news. It had utterly broken her heart. Carlie had so much potential, and the world seemed a much darker place after she died. She tried not to imagine her friend, her confidante, lying broken on the beach. She could almost see her tan skin framed by the beach pebbles, her coiled hair spread out around her beautiful face. Samuel interrupted her reverie.

"Listen, Maggie, I have serious reservations about this, but I know you're determined to talk to this source." Samuel turned to her, staring intently into her eyes. Maggie was struck by the warmth of their dark depths. "At least let me do some research for you. Give me the source's number and I'll run a trace on it. I still have buddies in the Bureau."

"Still? You're not there anymore?" Maggie was confused.

"I'm still a criminal profiler. At least, for now." Questions bubbled up in Maggie's mind, but before she had a chance to ask any of them, Samuel cut her off. "We can talk about all that later. Let me do some background digging while you're talking to this person. I'm sure you can use any extra information."

"Okay," said Maggie reluctantly. "The source was texting from a blocked number, though." As a journalist, the idea of giving up information about her sources went against everything she stood for. As a woman in a vulnerable situation, however, she wanted any and all protections available to her.

"There still might be a way to trace it. It'll depend on the level of encryption and how cooperative the telecommunications company is, but let me at least try," Samuel implored. Maggie trusted Samuel and nodded. She showed him the number, and he typed it into his phone.

They stood in silence together, shoulder to shoulder. There was no sign of any people. The only sounds were the warbling of birds and whispering of waves on the shore. The peaceful sounds belied the potentially dangerous situation Maggie was walking into. She felt, again, a wave of unease. How could such beautiful scenery be the backdrop to such tragedy?

"Are you *sure* you don't want me to come with you?" Samuel asked again.

"I'm sure," Maggie replied firmly. She knew Samuel thought she was taking an unnecessary risk, but she couldn't do anything to jeopardize getting this information about Carlie.

"I really don't like this." Samuel paused, then sighed at Maggie's resolute expression. "Fine. I'll go and wait over there." He pointed toward some large rocks jutting up on the opposite side of the rocky beach. "If anyone arrives it won't be as easy to see me, but I'll still be close enough to help you if anything happens."

"Nothing's going to happen," Maggie said, but she wasn't sure she believed that herself. She reached out and clasped Samuel's hand briefly. Seeing him stirred up emotions in her she thought she'd left in her past. She had put her relationship with Samuel in the *too-hard* category after leaving Vargo. She felt guilty for not returning the multiple calls and emails he'd made at first, and when he stopped trying she told herself it was a relief. She didn't want anything that reminded her of home, of what she had lost. She pulled away before she could get drawn any further into the moment. "I'll see you soon."

"I've got your back, Mags," Samuel said. She smiled and began walking toward the boathouse, adjusting her poncho and pulling her unruly hair back into a bun. Samuel strode in the direction of the rocks he'd pointed to.

The door to the boathouse had fallen off long ago, leaving the entrance wide open. Swallowing hard to moisten her dry throat, Maggie cautiously entered. Inside, she could see that the roof sagged under the weight of years of neglect, with missing shingles allowing glimpses of the sky to peek through. The air was heavy with the scent of neglect, the floor littered with debris. She could see from the crushed cans and cigarette butts that people had once hung out here, but it currently appeared empty to her.

"Hello?" she called. There was no response, just a silence that sent a chill through her. She looked up at the sky through the holes in the roof and saw swallows darting to and fro, the shadows of clouds passing over her upturned face. Her heart pounded in her chest, a staccato drumbeat marking the silent seconds passing. She could feel her hands trembling slightly and plunged them into the pockets of her pants. The sound of her own breathing echoed in the empty space.

She stepped farther into the building, noting that even though the structure was small there were still many places to hide behind upturned crates and wood. "Hello?" she called again, louder this time. Nothing. Every creak of the decaying wood sent shivers down her spine, and she glanced nervously back toward the entrance, half expecting to see the source approaching.

Get it together, she thought to herself sternly. She'd been in dicier situations than this before. She had covered the crime beat for a couple of different media outlets in LA, and she prided herself on her courage and steel nerves. She couldn't understand why this situation was getting to her so badly. She headed back toward the door, eager to be out of the shadows.

Eager, that was, until she saw movement between the trees, and the gray glint of a firearm pointed at her.

Samuel tried to call his Bureau colleague to pass on the number of Maggie's informant, but there was no service on his phone. It would have to wait until they got back to Vargo. He stepped farther behind the rocks and crouched down on his haunches. From this position he'd be able to see anyone approaching and quickly hide himself. He crossed his arms against his chest, trying to quell the unease growing inside him.

Everything about this felt wrong, and he wished Maggie had agreed to let him accompany her. Samuel respected strong women, and Maggie was one of the strongest he knew. However, at that moment he would have really appreciated a little less stubbornness.

He continually scanned the fields and tree line opposite his vantage point, his police training kicking in. He tensed as he thought he saw a flicker of movement between the tree trunks, about eighty yards away. He had just begun to doubt himself when he saw it again—someone was definitely moving in those trees. Was it Maggie's contact? He crouched low, his heart pounding in his chest like a war drum. Through the underbrush and pine branches, Samuel spotted the glint of a scope among the distant trees. Whoever it was, they had a gun.

His FBI instincts kicked into overdrive. He assessed his surroundings with cool precision, formulating the best way to make it to the boathouse. With seasoned expertise he began to move. Keeping his body low, he dashed from the rocks, staying close to the rocks next to him to avoid detection.

Without warning, he heard the sharp crack of a bullet and the splinter of wood as it hit the other side of the building, followed by a scream from Maggie. He resisted the urge to call out to her, not wanting to give up his position. He sprinted the rest of the way. *Lord, protect her right now*, he prayed silently. Reaching the boathouse, he pressed himself up against the wall, his refined awareness alert for further threat. Adrenaline coursed through his veins, heightening all his senses. Suddenly, he saw movement in the tree line, farther back from where he'd just left. He froze, wondering if he'd been seen. No more bullets flew through the air, but he knew there were at least two assailants in the woods above the beach.

He considered his next move. The window next to him had the glass smashed out of the frame. With ease, Samuel hauled his lithe body up over the frame and dropped into a crouch on the damp floor. He blamed himself for not bringing a weapon with him, but he had been hesitant to carry a gun during his leave of absence. There hadn't been any need for it at the cabin. With practiced breathing he steadied himself, knowing there was no point dwelling on what he'd *wished* he'd done. Instead, he rose from the floor and, keeping low, gazed around the edges of the structure.

"Maggie!" he whispered. He couldn't see any sign of her, but above the door a whole chunk of the frame had been shot off. The air was thick with grime and the musty scent of decay. Clouds of dust puffed up with each step of his Timberlands. "Maggie?" he called again, louder this time, unable to disguise the concern in his voice.

Samuel's keen eyes caught a flicker of movement in the shadows, to the right of the damaged door. He paused, and this time he saw Maggie's head peek around a stack of rotting wooden crates, directly in front of an empty window frame. Seeing him, she stood up. "Samuel!" she called. Before he could warn her to stay down, a series of shots rang out. Maggie threw herself flat on the floor.

Samuel also ducked low and ran closer to Maggie. Crouching behind an ancient rowboat draped in cobwebs, he stretched out his hand to her. "Maggie, crawl over to me. Stay as low to the ground as you can."

"I can't!" She was trembling, lying on her side to avoid putting pressure on her injured arm.

"Maggie, you can do this. Just take my hand." Samuel stretched farther toward her. He kept listening for sounds outside of the boathouse but heard only silence. Even the birds had quieted. "I've got your back. It's going to be okay."

She stretched out her hand to him and he grasped it firmly. Samuel pulled her over to him and they tucked themselves behind the boat. He pulled Maggie close to him and she buried her head in his shoulder.

"I'm so sorry. This is all my fault!" Maggie was sobbing. Samuel felt a wave of protectiveness break over him, and he tightened his arms around her shoulders. Her hair tickled his nose, and he could smell the crisp apple shampoo she used. Her fingers dug into his shoulder blades as she gripped on to him desperately.

"It's okay, it's okay," he soothed. He pushed her back a little, using one hand to bring her chin up so their eyes met. Tears swam in hers, catching the light and refracting their deep cobalt hues into a million tiny diamonds.

"Maggie, we're going to be fine. I'm going to keep you safe. I need you to listen to me and follow what I say. Can you do that?"

"Yes," she said. She took a shaky breath and tucked a stray russet curl behind her ear.

"You're doing great. Hold my hand and do not let go." He took a moment to survey the boathouse. How were they going to get out of here? The front door was out of the question, considering the position of the snipers. They could try the windows, but that might be slow since they both needed to climb out. His searching eyes landed on a narrow opening in the far wall where some of the boards had rotted away. It would position them away from the snipers and then he could figure out the next step.

"Follow me." Holding hands, they crouched down and darted toward the gap. Another shot rang out. The bullet sped through the empty window and struck the wall perilously close to their heads. *This guy is a professional*, Samuel noted silently.

The opening was small, but they both squeezed through, causing more of the boards to fall apart. The welcome fresh air cleared Samuel's mind. Ahead of them was the ocean, and he could see his boat. They would be sitting ducks if they tried to escape that way. He turned to the side and saw that low tide had revealed a narrow rock ledge around the side of the cliff. If they could make their way along that, they should be able to find the entrance of the caves.

"The ledge," Maggie said, and Samuel realized she'd seen it, too. They looked at each other and nodded wordlessly, intuitively understanding their next step. Holding hands, they raced from the protection of the boathouse. Every second was agony as Samuel waited for a bullet to hit them. They had made it just around the corner of the cliff and onto the ledge when several shots caused more of the boathouse to explode behind them.

Samuel led the way along the ledge. There was just enough room for them to walk single file. The surface was slippery, and they had to slow down considerably. He could feel his heart pounding. If the snipers were locals, they would know exactly where he and Maggie were headed. He just had to pray that they had enough of a head start.

FOUR

Maggie struggled to keep her balance on the slimy rocks. She tried to slow her breathing and focus on putting one foot in front of the other. Samuel kept a fast pace ahead of her, nimble as a mountain goat, and just as she was about to beg him to slow down she saw the mouth of the cave gaping in the cliff ahead of them.

There were many breathtaking cave systems in the islands of the bay. The Labyrinth was the smaller and less well-known of these systems, meaning there were rarely tourists and only sometimes locals. The safety of the caves was questionable, and cave-ins had been known to happen. For now, it was worth the risk.

Maggie followed him into the mouth of the cave. Ocean water rushed inside in a fast stream but there was still room for them to stand side-by-side for now. Samuel patted down his back pants pocket and frowned.

"What is it?" Maggie asked.

"My phone. I think it slipped out of my pocket back at the beach." He groaned, pulling his empty front pockets inside out to double check. Nothing.

Maggie reached into her pocket and plucked out her own phone.

"There wasn't any reception back at the beach, but maybe we can make a phone call from here?" Samuel suggested.

Maggie scrolled through her contacts and brought up her editor's name. In the past, whenever she'd gotten into dicey situations on assignment, she'd always called Everett. She pressed the dial button and was met with nothing but beeps on the other end. She pulled her phone away from her face and checked the screen. No bars. "We definitely don't have any service."

"You should call 911," Samuel said, looking at her expectantly.

"I can't do that, Samuel," Maggie said.

"Even without reception, you should still be able to get through to 911," Samuel insisted, misunderstanding her reticence.

"No, Samuel. It's not that I *can't* call 911, it's that I *won't* call 911," Maggie clarified.

"Maggie, you've been run off the road, strangled and now shot at. At what point are you willing to call in experts to help?" Samuel's voice was exasperated, and his face was stormy with frustration.

"I have to give this more of a chance. This contact is the closest I've ever gotten to getting real information about Carlie. If they are on this island, I need to find them. I can't do anything to jeopardize this opportunity." She rubbed her arms, goosebumps rising on her skin in the chilly wind that was beginning to pick up, her hoodie and jacket providing scant protection from the elements. She wanted to get inside the cave, where at least she would be insulated from the wind. "And besides, I kind of *have* called in expert help." She looked at him and smiled hopefully.

"Me?" Samuel gave a short, barking laugh. "I'm not technically on active duty. I haven't even brought my own weapon."

"Your best weapon is up here," Maggie said, tapping the side of her head to indicate she was talking about his brain. Samuel had always been physically strong and commanding, but he was also whip-smart and adaptable. She trusted him more than almost anyone else she could think of in a situation like this.

"You're impossible," Samuel groaned, but she knew from his lightening expression that she had convinced him. He gazed at her a moment, then sighed. "I guess we're really going ahead with this."

"So, what next?" she asked, smiling thankfully.

"I suppose we have to try and make it to higher ground." Samuel paused and rubbed the back of his neck. It was a familiar gesture, something that signaled to Maggie that he was thinking hard. "From what I remember, the caves run right under this ridge and there's an egress point on the other side of the island. Trying to reach it overland could take a while, and we'd be exposed," Samuel mused. "If we get into the caves, I'm hoping we can hide out for a bit or make it to the other side of the island and flag down a boat. Hopefully there'll be someone out here even with the storm coming."

"Do you think we should go back and try and get your boat?" Maggie asked.

"The sniper would shoot us immediately." Samuel motioned straight ahead. "This is our best chance at getting off this island."

Maggie hated the idea of getting trapped in the caves during a storm, but she nodded and followed him in. Low tide had been around an hour ago, and she knew that the rocks they were walking on would soon disappear as the tide heightened.

"Do you think you'll be able to find the opening on the other side of the island?" Maggie asked nervously.

"I've done it once before, but it was a while ago. I can certainly try again. Besides, we can always double back if we get stuck." Samuel rubbed his chin, adding, "That's if the tide hasn't gotten too high, though."

"I can do this alone," Maggie said slowly, noting Samuel's trepidation and nerves. "They're not after you, Sam. If you head back toward the boathouse, you have a better chance of staying safe."

"That's not going to happen, Mags, and you know it." Samuel looked at her firmly and she started to laugh. "What's so funny?"

"No one has called me 'Mags' since…well, actually, you're the only one who has ever called me Mags." They paused and looked at each other. There was warmth in his eyes. Suddenly Samuel spun around and started running his fingers along the rock wall near the mouth of the cave.

"I wonder if it's still here," he muttered to himself as he pulled at the rocks.

"What are you looking for?" Maggie asked, bemused. He continued to move with utter concentration.

"Aha!" Samuel triumphantly pulled a very old, very

dirty plastic bag out from a small hole in the cave wall. "The last time I came here was the summer just after college, maybe six years ago. A buddy and I did some exploring, and when we came out we hid a little kit in case we wanted to come back and do it again. We didn't end up getting back here…but this might still be in working order."

Maggie stood next to him to peer inside the plastic bag. Under dust and chunks of dirt she could see two headlamps and a coiled length of rope. "You are *such* a Boy Scout," Maggie teased Samuel delightedly, smiling as his cheeks turned red. "Always be prepared!"

"You should be grateful that at least one of us is a Scout!" Samuel laughed. He pulled out one of the headlamps and pried open the battery section. "These are lithium, and they were fresh when I put them in. The shelf life is up to ten years, so they might still have a little juice in them." He put the batteries back in and pushed the power button. A faint light flickered and glowed.

"Let me try the other." Maggie pulled the other headlamp out of its decrepit bag. She pushed the button, but this time no light turned on.

"At least one is working," Samuel said.

Sudden squawking shocked them. Several gulls were circling the water outside, cawing loudly over the sounds of a boat engine buzzing in the distance. "What if that's my contact? Maybe we should go back out?" Maggie suggested.

"And what if it's more snipers?" Samuel retorted. "I think our best bet is to get through to the other side of the island and flag down help. We can't leave ourselves in a vulnerable situation."

"Fine," Maggie agreed bitterly. She could see the wisdom in Samuel's suggestion, but she hated feeling out of control. She knew she was going to have to open up and trust him.

"Let's go, I don't want to wait around and find out which one of us is correct," Samuel said, his mouth making a concerned line. Maggie strapped the nonworking headlamp on, just in case, and Samuel led her into the dusky cave. The light from Samuel's headlamp warded off some of the gloomy darkness as they walked inside, the sunshine from the outside world growing increasingly faint.

The cave system stretched out ahead of them, shadows preventing them from seeing more than a few feet ahead. The light danced over stalactites hanging down from the ceiling, pointed menacingly at them like extended fingers. Maggie held on to Samuel's hand tightly as she struggled to find her footing on the uneven ground. The air was cool and still, carrying with it a faint scent of damp earth. Their footsteps reverberated off the walls, creating an eerie symphony that played in their ears.

"Do you think they're close?" Maggie asked. Even with her voice at a whisper level, the cavernous space carried her voice and magnified it uncannily.

"I think we've got enough of a head start to keep some distance between us," Samuel responded, squeezing her hand reassuringly.

They walked forward slowly and silently. The ground was slippery, and the farther they advanced the tighter the space became. After a few minutes they had to walk single file, and the top of Samuel's head brushed against the rocky ceiling. Maggie took deep breaths to fend off the panic building in her chest. She had never liked tight spaces, and her claustrophobia had increased as she grew older.

"Tell me something about your life," Maggie said, needing to be distracted.

"My life?" Samuel turned to look back at her and must have seen the fear on her face. "Well, after I got my forensics and criminal justice degree, I got accepted into the FBI and I've been working there as an analyst ever since."

"I knew that," Maggie admitted. "Tell me more. Why are you back in Vargo?"

"I'm just taking some time off," Samuel replied vaguely.

"But *why* are you taking time off?" Maggie asked, trying not to turn this into an interrogation—though she'd never been very good at backing down when something had piqued her interest. As much as she knew Samuel loved his grandfather's cabin, she also knew his dream had always been to work for the FBI.

"That's a long story," Samuel said. His tone was evasive, and she knew he wasn't revealing the whole truth. "For the past nine months, though, I've been a real jack-of-all-trades. I totally gutted the cabin, painted everything, landscaped and even taught myself some plumbing. Turns out I really love working with my hands!"

"And what about your grandpa? Is he well?" Maggie

asked, realizing she hadn't seen any trace of him back at the cabin that morning.

"He died nine months ago. I inherited the cabin in his will." Samuel's voice was low and sad.

"Oh, Sam, I'm so sorry," Maggie said, squeezing his hand. She knew his grandpa had helped raise him and had been integral in creating the man Samuel had become—honest, honorable and trustworthy. "He was such a great man. Just like you."

"Thanks," Samuel said simply. They walked on in silence. She wondered what else had brought Samuel back to Vargo, but she knew it wasn't time to push further. Maybe it was a girlfriend? They'd known Jennifer Simms in high school—perhaps she'd been part of the reason he returned. And was it her imagination, or did Samuel have a slight limp? She felt regret churning in her stomach as she pondered these questions. She wished she hadn't pushed him away all those years ago.

She had considered telling him her true feelings back in high school, but after Carlie died she pushed everyone around her away, trying to bury her pain deep within—Samuel included. She had applied to UCLA on a whim, but when she was accepted, the distance from Vargo made it seem like the best choice for her. She wanted to run as far away as possible from everything that reminded her of her pain.

Though they'd only become close friends as seniors, she'd had a crush on Samuel since she first saw him in freshman year; the honor roll student and star quarterback on the football team. Even in high school he'd been exceptionally handsome, over six feet tall before his senior year with a shiny crop of raven black hair and the warmest chocolate eyes she'd ever seen. All the girls had been in love with him, and Maggie couldn't imagine he'd ever be interested in her.

Then they were placed in the same AP English class in senior year. The first day of class, Maggie sat at an empty seat in the back. She was a straight A soccer star and dancer, but she was very quiet. She preferred to listen and observe. She knew she wasn't beautiful in the way the popular girls were. She had copper curls that, even then, were wild unless she kept them pulled back into her habitual ponytail. She was petite and pale, never managing a tan even during the hottest parts of summer. Though she'd come to love the constellation of freckles on her face, in high school she hated them with a passion. The popular girls had smooth tanned skin, hair straightened so that it flowed down their backs like a waterfall and legs that seemed to stretch on forever. Pretty much the opposite of her.

She was shocked when Samuel chose to come and sit next to her on that first day of class, even though there were other open seats. He had smiled at her, and her heart had somersaulted. That was the beginning of their friendship—and her love for him. And she had never told him.

She pushed those recollections to the back of her mind as her shoulder grazed against the rough cave wall. She was resolute: this was not the time in her life for love or relationships. Her work required everything from her, and she wasn't willing to open herself up in a way that left her vulnerable to pain.

As they wormed their way deeper into the bowels

of the cave system, she could feel her chest becoming tighter and her breathing shallower. If there was anyone behind them right now, they were completely trapped. There was no room to even turn around and try to defend themselves.

Drops of ice cold water fell from the damp ceiling, trickling through her curls and down her neck. She felt as if she were one step away from falling into a ravine of panic. Samuel's warm grasp on her hand was the only thing keeping her tethered to the reality of what they were doing: They were here for Carlie.

Maggie swallowed the terror that was threatening to rip its way from her throat and put one step in front of the other. She had to keep moving, despite the peril that lay before them—and behind them.

After what felt like miles of pushing through a claustrophobic section of tunnel, it finally began to widen and soon they emerged into a cavern, replete with stalactites and stalagmites. A thin stream of salt water had followed them into the cave, and now it expanded into a large pool. Samuel realized that if this was what the caves looked like at low tide, there would be a whole lot more water at high tide. *Please help us get out of here before the tide comes in*, he prayed.

The atmosphere of the cave was oppressive and ominous. The cavern yawned open like the mouth of a hungry animal and the stalactites were hanging like crooked, dangerous teeth. The air was thick with dampness and the pools of stagnant water on the uneven floor emanated damp, rotten scents. The darkness was pierced only by a hole in the ceiling and Samuel's headlamp, illuminating the walls slick with moisture and mineral veins.

Despite the hole far above them allowing the sunshine to filter in, it was still cold. He could feel goosebumps prickling his skin. He took a moment to pause and evaluate their surroundings. On the opposite side of the pool of water he could see another tunnel, but from what he remembered he needed to continue straight, where a different tunnel branched off the cavern.

"Do you know where we are?" Maggie asked. She looked up at him, biting her lip nervously. He couldn't remember her ever really showing fear before. Even when Carlie had died, she hadn't allowed herself to be vulnerable, keeping her distance and not allowing him in.

"I think so. We need to keep going straight, as far as I remember." He readjusted the rope where he had looped it over his shoulder. "Do you want to rest for a couple of minutes before we keep going?"

"Yes," Maggie said, plopping gratefully onto a nearby outcropping of rock that extended from the cavern wall, forming a natural table-like surface. She turned her face up to be bathed in the sun, and strands of fire stood out in her curls. Samuel swallowed and turned away.

He cocked his head to the side and listened. There was the sound of dripping water, a steady cadence that threaded through the silence. Was he imagining things, or could he hear distant rocks shifting back from the direction they'd come from? Could the snipers have found the cave? The urge to keep moving made him restless, but Maggie had drawn her knees up to her chest, resting her forehead against them. She was exhausted. He decided it was safe enough to catch their breath for a moment.

"This is insane." Her voice was muffled, but Samuel could hear desperation in Maggie's words.

"That's an understatement," Samuel said. He was edgy, pacing along the damp rocks beside the pool of water. "Do you think one of those men is your source?"

"I think it has to be connected to Carlie." Maggie's voice was clearer now. She was sitting up straight, her face pale but resolute. "My source knew so much about Carlie's death. But do you think they would have played a long game like that? Engaged in online discussions with me for months just to lure me here?"

"I think someone lured you here to hurt you, but I'm not sure this is ultimately about Carlie." Samuel thought aloud. "Are you sure it's not something else? Any of the other cases you've covered or sources you've met? If you've upset the wrong person, maybe they are using your online hunt for Carlie to get to you."

"I don't think so. I mean, I've met some bad people over the years, but I always protect my sources and I haven't worked an active case in years. I've mainly been focused on cold cases. Why would they wait this long to exact revenge?" Maggie stood up. "It has to be Carlie. It can't be a coincidence."

"Hmm." Samuel was noncommittal. As an analyst, he was used to digging deep under the surface and he never took things at face value. However, over the years he had learned that Occam's razor generally applied—the simplest explanation is more likely to be the correct one. Why would someone be trying to cover up the death of a high schooler in Vargo from over a decade ago? It seemed much likelier that Maggie had made enemies when she was a crime reporter.

"You think it's something else?" Maggie must have picked up on his hesitancy. "You don't believe me?"

"It's not about me believing you or not. I just… I have more experience than you with these things, and I'm not sure that this is about Carlie." Samuel could have kicked himself. As soon as the words came out of his mouth, he knew he was coming off like a know-it-all.

"Oh yes, I forgot. Mr. FBI." Maggie was fuming. "I don't need you to mansplain this situation to me, thank you very much. In case you forgot, I have years of investigative experience myself."

"Okay, okay." Samuel held up his hands in surrender. He couldn't help but notice that she was almost regal in her fury, the very hairs on her head seeming to crackle with rage like an indignant crown. He was about to apologize when there was an echo from the caves in the direction they'd come in. He and Maggie both shot around to look.

"Let's go," Samuel said after a moment. He led the way along the cavern wall and into the tunnel straight ahead. He moved at a faster pace now, feeling uneasy, almost like prey being hunted in the darkness. The dim light from his headlamp was flickering, and he knew the battery wouldn't hold out much longer. As they ran, Samuel tried to listen for sounds other than their footfalls and ragged breaths. He could have sworn he could hear thumps behind them, rocks shifting, but he didn't want to stop and investigate.

“What’s that?” Maggie asked. They had been jogging for maybe five minutes, their breathing quickened from the rapid pace. Samuel lowered the headlight beam and could make out a pinprick of light ahead, in the side of the tunnel. “Is that a hole?”

“Could be.” Hope invigorated him, and they nearly ran to reach it. Maggie had been correct. It was a small hole in the side of the cave, just big enough for Samuel to squeeze his broad shoulders through. He maneuvered his bulk out of the cave and turned around to pull Maggie through. They looked around.

They had come out in a heavily wooded area, and Samuel knew this wasn’t where they needed to be. “The exit must be farther up.” He put his hands on his hips with a groan, disappointment extinguishing his confidence.

“It’s okay. Let’s just get back in and keep walking.” The strained optimism in Maggie’s voice didn’t disguise her anxiety. “It can’t be much farther. Right?”

“Right.” Samuel hoped he sounded convincing. For a moment they considered the tunnel, loath to leave the sunlight for its dim interior. With a sigh, Maggie wordlessly strode back over and slipped back inside. Samuel was close behind when he heard the sharp intake of her breath.

“Sam!”

He nearly dove back inside the tunnel. It took a second for his eyes to adjust, even with the aid of the headlamp, but he felt fear grip his chest once he knew what he was seeing.

Two masked men flanked Maggie, one with a gun trained on her, the other with a gun pointed right at his head.

FIVE

"Don't move." One of the snipers jabbed his rifle at Samuel, who was frozen near the cave opening. Maggie saw his eyes darting between the attackers and could tell he was internally weighing the risk of disarming them. When he raised his hands in acquiescence, she knew he had decided there wasn't a safe way to try overpowering the men.

"Give that to me." The same sniper nodded at the rope that Samuel still had looped over his shoulder. Samuel let it slide off his shoulder and passed it to him. The sniper looped it over his own shoulder. "Step toward me. *Slowly.*"

Samuel followed the orders. He made eye contact with Maggie and whispered, "I've got your back."

"Shut up." It was the other sniper this time. His voice was hoarse and low, and Maggie recognized from its tenor that he was the same person who had attacked her at the gas station. She looked at him and saw his unsettling blue eyes. Both men wore black sweatshirts with the hoods drawn over their heads and gaiter masks drawn up over their noses. Blue Eyes was bigger than she'd first realized—nearly six feet tall with a solid bulkiness that came from hours in the gym. The other sniper was several inches shorter and reedier. Who *were* these men?

"Are you going to kill us?" Maggie blurted out, her eyes locked on Blue Eyes's gun. She'd been close to guns before. She'd even learned to shoot at her parents' small farm growing up, but these guns were different. They glowed dully in the low light, ghastly and threatening. Considering they'd tried their hardest to kill them both back at the boathouse, she couldn't understand why they hadn't shot them when they'd reentered the cave. "You were certainly trying your best to kill us when we were back at the beach."

"Our orders have changed." Blue Eyes threw a short strand of rope at Samuel, who caught it deftly. "Tie her hands." He motioned his head at Maggie. Samuel hesitated, looking between the sniper and Maggie. "*Do it*," Blue Eyes hissed, prodding Samuel with the butt of his rifle.

"It's okay, Sam," Maggie said, extending her hands. Samuel's expression was full of an apoplectic anger, his jaw set so hard it was a wonder he wasn't cracking his teeth. Maggie kept her eyes trained on the ground as Samuel tied her wrists together loosely.

"Tighter." It was the other sniper this time. His voice was less hoarse than Blue Eyes, and he sounded younger. Samuel pulled the rope tighter and then extended his hands to Maggie to tie his. She took a length of rope from Blue Eyes and bound Samuel's hands with shaking fingers. Once the snipers were satisfied with her work, they pushed her in front and began walking.

Blue Eyes walked beside her, one hand clasping her upper arm, the other balancing his rifle. His grip was painful, and she could imagine lilac bruises expanding under his fingers to match the ones around her throat. *Our orders have changed.* The words reverberated in her mind. Who was giving them orders? What threat was Maggie posing to these men? "Why are you doing this?" she asked after a moment.

"You should have minded your business," was Blue Eyes's curt response. "Now keep your mouth shut and walk." She could hear Samuel's footsteps behind her, matching pace with the other sniper who was guarding him. Both men switched on flashlights attached to their rifles, but even with the additional illumination Maggie kept stumbling over the slippery rocks that littered the uneven ground. Both snipers walked confidently, and she got the sense they were familiar with the terrain.

She knew she had to try and engage the men. She wanted them to see her and Samuel as human beings, rather than targets to be captured. Though she had been quiet in high school, throughout college and her journalism career she had learned how to confidently harness her voice to connect with people. Her work depended on asking the right questions, having the right conversations and connecting with the right people. She took a deep breath and said, "You must be locals, you seem to know this area well. Samuel and I both grew up here."

Neither of the men acknowledged her. She tried again. "I must have done something to really annoy you. The problem is, I have no idea what it is. Can you help me out?" Silence. "There's still time to fix this. Let us go, and we can all go back to our lives. You don't want to spend the rest of your life in a prison cell just for 'following orders.'"

Without warning, Blue Eyes rounded on Maggie, pressing the barrel of the gun against her temple. The sudden fear that cut through her sharpened her senses to a pinpoint. She was painfully aware of the cold metal pressed against her skin and the way her breath caught and quickened. Fear tangled with disbelief. Her heart pounded in her chest, a violent rhythm.

"I told you to stay quiet and walk. You should be grateful to be alive right now, but I can end your life at any moment." He was breathing heavily now, fury rippling through his words. He'd seemed calm and in control just moments ago, and Maggie knew she'd gotten to him. She swallowed the acrid terror that burned her throat, knowing that she had to keep pushing if they wanted to know the truth.

"If your orders have changed, that means someone wants us alive. Can you tell me who that is?" Maggie asked, turning to face Blue Eyes. She hoped she sounded more assured than she was. She clenched her hands to try and stop them from quaking. "Is this about Carlie Rodriguez?"

"Maggie, stop," Samuel said sharply. At the same moment, Blue Eyes turned to face her and lifted his rifle. He slammed the butt of his gun into her temple, and Maggie felt a sharp explosion of pain before she fell to the ground. The force of the blow sent shockwaves through her skull, shaking her consciousness like a baby's rattle.

She must have passed out briefly, because when she

forced her eyes open she saw Samuel grappling with one of the snipers in the tunnel ahead of her. By the size of the man she could tell it was Blue Eyes. She looked around wildly and saw the other sniper lying opposite her, his head slumped to the side and blood running from his nose.

When she looked back she saw Blue Eyes had pinned Samuel to the ground, his rifle pressed horizontally across Samuel's throat in an attempt to crush his windpipe. Maggie struggled to move but a wave of dizziness pinned her back to the ground, leaving her balancing on the edge of an abyss of unconsciousness.

Lord, give me strength, she prayed quietly. She took several deep, steadying breaths and gingerly pushed herself onto her hands and knees. Her vision flickered at the edges but she fought the dizziness. A steady beat of pain kept pace in her temple, but she forced herself to crawl forward. Samuel's movements were slowing, and she knew his tied hands were stopping him from defending himself against the pressure of the rifle.

Maggie desperately searched around her for a makeshift weapon. Her cinched hands landed on a large, jagged rock. She grasped it firmly and stood on wobbly legs. Over and over the words *Lord, guide me* sang through her head, and she weaved her way unsteadily toward the men scrabbling on the damp floor. Almost without thinking, Maggie raised the rock above her head and brought it down with all her might on Blue Eyes's skull.

A sharp crack reverberated through the tunnel, and the sniper slumped over, releasing the pressure on the rifle. Samuel used the last ounce of his strength to push him away and then Maggie grabbed one of his arms and pulled him into a sitting position. He took desperate, greedy gulps of air, feeling the pain in his lungs abate and this mind clear.

"Are you okay?" Maggie was peering into his face. The weak light from his headlamp showed blood smeared from her right temple down to her jaw. The flesh where she'd been hit was already beginning to swell.

"I'm fine, but you're not!" Samuel brought his bound hands up to her chin, turning it to get a better look at her wound. "That looks nasty."

"I'll be fine," Maggie said brusquely, brushing his hands away. She sat back down on the ground and peered around her. She suddenly moved over to the sniper, collapsed on the cold ground next to them. "Oh no, is he… is he dead?"

Samuel crouched down next to the man. After a few seconds he heard a ragged breath, then another. "He's breathing." Samuel stood and felt along the wall of the tunnel until his fingers touched a sharp outcrop. He rubbed the rope binding his wrists against it tightly and soon it snapped and fell to the ground. Wordlessly he guided Maggie over and helped her to do the same.

Their hands now free, Samuel pulled the gun away from one assailant and walked back down the tunnel to retrieve the other sniper's rifle. "Can you hold these?" Samuel pressed the rifles into Maggie's hands. She was shaking, staring at the man she'd knocked out. "Maggie?" Samuel could see she was in shock, her breathing rapid and shallow. "*Maggie?*"

"Yeah," she said finally, still staring at the sniper.

"Maggie, look at me." Samuel's voice was clinical and commanding. He was in survival mode now, his instincts screaming at him to get them to safety. She finally wrenched her eyes away from the unconscious man and met Samuel's gaze. "Good. I need you to keep breathing, slowly. Stand here and don't move."

Once Maggie's breathing had slowed down, Samuel walked over to the smaller of the snipers. When Maggie was hit, Samuel had had a split second to make a choice. Harnessing his finely tuned instincts, he had rapidly driven his elbow into his captor's nose, then his throat. With brutal force he'd used both cinched hands to drive the man's head into the side of the tunnel before he ran forward and attacked the other sniper, who quickly pinned him. If Maggie hadn't incapacitated the man, he wasn't sure he would have been able to overpower him.

Getting a firm grasp beneath his armpits, Samuel dragged the smaller man over to lie next to the larger sniper. He took the rope the man had confiscated and, using a series of quick knots, tied the two men together—back-to-back and lying on their sides. The knots wouldn't hold them forever, but it would delay them if they were to try and escape. He made sure their airways were clear and they were breathing before patting down their pockets. The smaller man had a walkie-talkie strapped to his back pocket, and Samuel clipped it to his own pants.

Turning back to Maggie, he saw she was still frozen to the spot, the rifles shaking slightly in her hands. He walked up to her and carefully took one of the rifles from her. He moved the bolt handle up and kicked out the ammunition inside, before removing the magazine and emptying it. He threw the empty magazine and rifle to the side and emptied the other one. Stowing the ammunition in his pockets, he kicked both rifles down the tunnel a little but didn't bother hiding them. Without ammo, they were useless, and they were too big and bulky to bother taking with them.

"Are you sure he's going to survive?" Maggie asked as Samuel returned to her. He pulled her into a tight hug and felt her hands grip on to his shirt like he was rescuing her from drowning.

"Yes. Both their airways are clear, they're lying in the recovery position and they're breathing." Samuel pulled back and grasped her shoulders. "Maggie, we have to go. Now. I don't know how long they'll be out, or how long the rope will restrain them."

"Wait." Maggie broke free and crouched next to the men. She pulled their gaiter masks down and motioned Samuel over. "Do you recognize either of them?"

He crouched down so his headlamp illuminated the smaller man's face. His sharp intake of breath echoed in the tunnel. He definitely recognized the man—his face was pale and angular, with sharp, narrow features. His cheeks were slightly sunken, giving him a gaunt, almost fragile look. Small, beady eyes sat beneath wiry, unkempt eyebrows, and his nose was thin and slightly hooked.

"Jake Boyd," he muttered. Ignoring Maggie's questioning look, he moved over to the larger man and peered into his face. "And Ryan Thatcher." In direct contrast to Boyd, Thatcher's face was broad and square, with a thick jawline that seemed almost too pronounced. His skin was rough, tanned and pockmarked from years of intense physical strain; veins bulged under his skin, especially around his forehead. His features were exaggerated—a testament to both years of aggression and chemical influence, likely steroids.

"How do you know them?" Maggie asked. "I grew up here, too, and they're not familiar to me."

"They're mainland transplants. They moved here after you left. I know them through friends. Vargo is still small enough that you definitely notice those who didn't grow up here." Samuel sighed as the full impact of what he was seeing hit him. "And they're cops. They transferred here, if I remember correctly."

Maggie was silent, and when he looked up she was shaking her head. "So I was right—we can't trust the cops."

"We can't trust *these* cops," Samuel corrected. "I still have contacts we can rely on. We just have to get out of here and find somewhere to hunker down so I can make some calls." Maggie pulled her phone out of her pocket again and immediately shook her head. No reception still.

"We could go back out the way we came—head to your boat?" Maggie suggested.

"I think the ledge might be underwater. It's only exposed for a short window, basically at low tide and an hour or so on either side of that." Samuel rubbed the back of his neck. "Let's try going out through the crack we found. We can climb down to the beach and take my boat back to Vargo. We still have another half hour or so before the storm hits."

"That sounds like a good plan." Maggie looked as relieved as Samuel felt. Walking back through the caves as the tide rose was the last thing he wanted to do. They took one last look at the men, still unconscious, and squeezed back out of the cave.

Outside, clouds were beginning to gather, dark and menacing. Samuel felt urgency tingle in his limbs, but he stood quietly for a moment to get his bearings. They had emerged into a clearing on a ridge, near the edge of the cliff. The island rose higher still above them, but he could make out a narrow dirt path in the trees ahead of them. Maggie spoke first.

"Looks like a path, maybe it leads down to the bay?"

"Let's try it," Samuel replied. They silently treaded the path together. Samuel hadn't been to church in years, hadn't prayed to or relied on God, but the last twenty-four hours had renewed a sense of connection for him. He felt close to God as he walked into the forest.

His time in the Bureau had taught him to remain calm under extreme circumstances. Part of his training required him to learn techniques to ground him in the moment. He used that knowledge now, sharpening his senses. The towering junipers, white oaks and pines closed around them, and he was in awe of their majesty. He breathed deeply, inhaling the earthy scent from the forest, noticing the hints of moss, decayed leaves and wet soil. He could hear the ocean coming closer, and the path they walked was heading down.

"I think we're on the right track," he said, peering behind him. Maggie was walking close, holding her injured wrist against her chest. She smiled and nodded at him, though he noticed she looked drawn. "How's your head?"

"It's fine," she responded quickly. It looked like the blood had stopped, but the side of her face was still caked in red and it was hard to gauge the severity of the damage. Samuel noticed a small brook running through the trees parallel to them.

"Let me quickly clean your wound. I want to make sure it's not too serious," he said. They walked a few feet into the tree line and stopped at the stream. Samuel dipped his hand into the crystal clear depths and drew some of the water to his lips. "It's clean." In a series of quick movements, he scooped water onto Maggie's face, using the sleeve of his jacket to gently remove some of the blood. She winced but didn't pull away.

"So, what's the verdict, doc? Am I gonna make it?" Maggie joked grimly once the area had been cleaned.

"It's bruised and swollen, but I don't think you need stitches," Samuel said, cupping her jaw tenderly and studying the injury.

"Good. Let's keep going. I don't want to be on this island when Boyd and Thatcher wake up," Maggie said.

They walked the rest of the way down the trail in silence. It was steep toward the end, and they had to slide down the very last part, holding on to tree roots to steady themselves. Samuel heard Maggie's sigh of relief as they finally made it to the beach.

Ahead of them, Samuel could see his motorboat where he had left it, pulled up above the waves on the rocky shore. "Look!" Maggie said, pointing to where the other boat they'd seen had been sitting. It was gone. Samuel thought back to the engine sounds they'd heard earlier—the men must have used the boat to access the cave.

"At least mine's still here," Samuel said. They scrambled over to it and Samuel pushed it into the water, Maggie assisting with one hand. Just as it hit the water, Samuel stopped. "No!" he hissed.

He hauled the boat back up out of the water and ran around to take a closer look at the outboard motor. He could see now that it was riddled with bullet holes. He tried desperately to turn it on, but it remained silent and still.

"Sam, look." He turned and saw Maggie pointing at the bottom of the boat. Water was pooled in the bottom where more bullet holes had pierced the aluminum floor.

They were stranded. Their only means of escape, short of swimming an impossibly long distance, was destroyed. If they didn't find another way to get off this island, they would be sitting ducks. He needed to think fast, or his and Maggie's lives were in danger.

SIX

Maggie stared forlornly at the ocean water pooling in the bottom of the boat. She looked up at the sky and noticed dark rain clouds were crowding the sun. The temperature had dropped.

"Thatcher and Boyd must have shot up the boat when we were running to the cave," Samuel said quietly. He sighed deeply and pulled the boat all the way back up the beach.

"What are we going to do?" Maggie asked. She looked out into the bay. There were no boats, and the waves were beginning to get choppy. She knew their window for safely leaving was closing.

"I'm going to try and radio for help," Samuel said, holding up the walkie-talkie he'd taken from Boyd. It was a heavy-duty waterproof model, and it looked military or police issue to Maggie. She'd known many police officers who carried similar kinds.

"Do you think it's a good idea to broadcast our position?" Maggie asked. She looked around as if she half expected someone to jump out from behind the rocks.

"What if Boyd and Thatcher were using it to communicate with whoever else was in on the plan?"

"We are also stranded on an island with a storm approaching," Samuel pointed out. He studied the unit in his hand for a moment. "Those guys are cops, and this looks like a police issue radio. I think we should take the chance to radio for help. What do you think?"

Maggie looked at Samuel, appreciating that he was respectful enough to ask her opinion. She nodded hesitantly. "You're right. This is probably worth the risk."

Samuel lifted the radio up to his mouth. He pressed a button and said loudly, "Mayday, mayday. Can anyone hear me? Over."

There was a pause and some static crackled. Samuel tried again, repeating his mayday. Suddenly, a voice burst over the speaker. "Boyd, is that you? Go ahead with your mayday. Over."

Samuel stared at the walkie-talkie. Maggie could feel her heart pick up speed. Whoever was on the other end of the radio was expecting a call from one of their attackers. Had they helped them plan the kidnapping?

"Sam, wait," Maggie said, covering Samuel's hand with hers before he responded. "Whoever is on the other end is expecting you to be Boyd. We can't risk that person being in on Boyd and Thatcher's plan and knowing we escaped."

"Why don't I ask who is on the other end?" Samuel asked, ignoring the repeated request to relay their mayday.

"Then they'd know you're not Boyd!" Maggie said. "I think you should pretend to be Boyd. Say your boat isn't working and you need emergency evacuation. We can see who comes to the beach and decide then whether it's safe to trust them."

"Okay, let's try that." Samuel nodded. He lifted the receiver to his mouth. "This is Boyd. We are having engine issues with our boat and can't leave South Rock Island. We're requesting an emergency evacuation. Over."

"Mayday received, Boyd. Have you managed to apprehend the targets? Over."

Maggie and Samuel shared a wide-eyed look. She felt a surge of relief that they hadn't revealed who they were. Whoever this person was, they wanted her and Samuel taken down. She was sure it must have something to do with Carlie.

"Targets have been apprehended. Can you confirm evacuation? Over," Samuel said.

"All boat travel has been suspended due to the impending storm. I'll do my best to get out to you. In the meantime, take cover and wait for my next instructions. Over and out."

"Understood. Over and out." Samuel clipped the walkie-talkie back to his pants and turned to Maggie. "You were right, they have a direct line to whoever is helping orchestrate this attack."

"At least they think you and I are restrained, rather than the other way around. We have the element of surprise now," Maggie said. She rubbed the back of her neck and looked up at the sky as fat raindrops began to fall from the heavy clouds.

"So now we wait until we see who turns up, I guess. Maybe there'll be a way to restrain them, too, and take their boat back to the mainland." Samuel pulled the hood of his jacket over his head. "Honestly, I'm still confused about why they were trying to restrain us now, when they wanted to kill you this morning."

"I have the same question." Maggie drew her own hood up as the rain came down harder. "Where can we take cover? I don't think it's safe to be in the caves right now."

"Let's go up to the ridge. I went hunting here years ago, and there was an old shack that we used. It might still be there. There are too many holes in the boathouse roof. I don't think it would offer much shelter." Samuel pointed up in the direction they'd just walked down. Maggie nodded and followed Samuel back up the hill.

The path was already slippery from the rain, and Maggie had to use tree roots to physically haul herself up at times. She struggled to keep her footing on loose rocks, scrabbling in the mud until Samuel offered his hand to support her. The path dried out a little as it threaded through the trees, the leaves offering some protection from the rain, but it was still hard going, and Maggie was breathing rapidly when they finally emerged on the ridge line.

The temperature had continued to drop, and Maggie could feel goosebumps prickling her arms even after the strenuous hike. They stood together, looking out over the bay, waves churning as the wind picked up. She realized they were still holding hands, but made no move to let go. The air felt charged somehow. She wasn't sure if that was from the storm or the electricity passing between their hands.

"Looks like it's going to be a big one," Samuel said,

gazing up again. The sky was now completely covered by dark clouds, their obsidian hues a warning sign. The rain kept falling, harder now, and as they looked up they heard thunder rumbling, followed by a flash of lightning.

"We need to get to that shelter," Maggie said urgently. Samuel nodded and led them away from the ridge and into a copse of trees. They continued to follow the dirt path, though at times it was so overgrown that Maggie almost couldn't see it. Finally a structure appeared ahead of them, surrounded by trees. Its wooden walls were warped and splintered but still standing and moss grew in patches along the bottom outer edges.

They dashed inside and Samuel pushed the door shut behind them, though the swollen wood wouldn't close the whole way. Inside was a rickety wooden table with two chairs, as well as a wooden bench running along one wall. It was otherwise bare. It smelled damp and musty, but at least it was dry. Maggie peeled off her sodden poncho and hung it on a hook on the wall. Samuel followed suit with his jacket.

"So now what?" Maggie asked as they looked at each other.

"We wait."

The rain beat a heavy rhythm on the tin roof above them, at times so loud they had to raise their voices to be heard. Samuel was sitting in one of the old wooden chairs, Maggie opposite him in the other. He had managed to scrounge up an old bottle of water stored beneath the bench, dusty but still sealed, and they shared it between them.

"I still can't believe Thatcher and Boyd are cops. Thatcher was the one that attacked me at the gas station and at the hospital, too, I'm sure of it," Maggie said.

"I'm shocked," Samuel said honestly. He didn't know either man well, but he was appalled that any law enforcement officers had been involved in trying to harm Maggie.

"Are you still convinced it has nothing to do with Carlie?" Maggie asked, her chin jutting out defiantly.

"I'm not convinced of anything," Samuel said. In truth, he was starting to see that Maggie's presence back at Vargo may have stirred up some trouble. He wondered whether she'd been lured back or whether nefarious individuals had found out she was coming back and wanted to stop her from learning more. "But why would people be trying to stop you finding out the truth about Carlie?"

"Maybe whoever killed her is still here and wants to make sure I don't find them," Maggie mused.

"What makes you so sure she was murdered?" Samuel asked.

"I have a copy of the coroner's report," Maggie admitted hesitantly.

"How did you manage that?" Samuel was impressed at her resourcefulness.

"Initially I only had her death certificate, and that lists her cause of death as an accidental drowning." Maggie leaned forward in her chair, her hands moving animatedly as she filled Samuel in. "But there were so many rumors that she didn't really drown, and nothing about the circumstances made sense. I don't know if you heard, but Carlie's grandparents raised her, and they moved to Montana after she died."

"I remember." Samuel nodded. His mother had been friends with Carlie's grandparents, and she had told Samuel about their decision to move to Missoula. "My mom told me they wanted a totally fresh start, that everything about Vargo reminded them of Carlie."

"Yeah, it was very hard for them." Maggie paused for a moment, frowning. "I tracked them down last year and went out to visit them. They're doing okay, for the most part, but when I told them about my investigation her grandma got really upset. She didn't want to dredge up old memories. I was walking out the door to leave when Carlie's grandpa stopped me. He gave me an envelope that had the coroner's report in it. Apparently he'd read some of my articles and remembered our friendship, and he said he trusted me to do the right thing by his granddaughter. He wanted me to investigate Carlie's death because he didn't believe she'd drowned, either.

"Anyway, the report noted that there were multiple lacerations and contusions found on Carlie's body but then it just brushes over that and lists her cause of death as asphyxiation due to drowning. It put her time of death as twelve to twenty-four hours prior to her body being discovered, and that never made sense to me. Her boyfriend, Shep, said he found a note from her that she'd left in his locker—that's apparently how he knew to go looking for her here on South Rock. She'd definitely arrived at school, but it seems like she skipped classes after lunch and never returned. Shep found her body around five p.m. That's a maximum of five hours between her leaving school and Shep finding her."

"That definitely doesn't line up with the coroner's report," Samuel agreed.

"Exactly!" Maggie gazed at him intensely. "I need to get more information. The report doesn't note if water was found in Carlie's lungs, and that would be an important indication of whether she was still alive when she went into the water."

"Once we get off the island, we should report all of this to the police," Samuel suggested. He could tell Maggie didn't like the idea, but she didn't say anything. "They can follow up with the coroner's office and get further information about the death."

"Sam, I know you have good relationships with law enforcement, and you have every reason to trust them. I mean, you are *in* the same industry, after all," Maggie said slowly. "Honestly, I've been covering cases like these for years, and I've seen how the police operate—too many times they're more interested in closing cases than actually solving them. If I hand over this evidence now, it'll either get buried or twisted to fit their narrative. I'm not risking it."

"I get it, Mags. I really do. But not all cops are corrupt." Samuel tried to keep the frustration out of his voice. He knew that Boyd and Thatcher hadn't made his case to go to law enforcement any stronger, but he also felt like this wasn't a situation they were equipped to deal with by themselves. "You can't just assume that every cop is part of the problem. If this goes to the right hands, it could help you solve Carlie's case."

"I hear what you're saying, Sam. Once I've met the source, I'll have more information to decide whether to get the police involved," Maggie said.

"But where is this anonymous source? We're stuck in this mess because you're following some harebrained scheme to meet up with a complete stranger, and now you're getting run off the road, strangled, shot at... Maggie, when are you going to wake up and see that you can't handle this by yourself?" Samuel could feel his voice rising as frustration and fear surged through him. All he wanted was to keep Maggie safe, but he couldn't do that if she refused to help herself.

"Sam, listen," Maggie said softly, reaching out and touching his arm. "I know you're trying to protect me, but I have to see this through. For Carlie. Once we get back to the mainland, I'm sure I'll be able to make contact with the source. They probably saw other people on the island and got spooked."

"This doesn't sit well with me, but I will support you seeing this through," Samuel said eventually. Maggie smiled and nodded, sitting back in her chair.

For a moment the only sound was the harsh rap of rain around them. Next to them was a tiny window, and Maggie gazed out of it now. The dim light that shone through seemed to make her skin glow. Her porcelain skin, copper hair and cerulean eyes all emitted a radiance. That inner brilliance was what had drawn Samuel to her all those years ago. Maggie was different from all the other girls he'd known. She was fiercely intelligent, independent and strong. She was a lot quieter in high school, but even then she never backed down from a fight for what she thought was right. She was unapologetically herself—even as a teenager, when social pressures forced so many of their peers to create facades.

Now, in the midst of danger and uncertainty, Maggie was sticking to her principles. Samuel was frustrated that they still hadn't called the police, but he couldn't help but feel admiration for Maggie's stance. She was determined to seek justice for her friend, and he was going to do what it took to support her.

Samuel thought back to the last conversation they had before she left town, the day of their high school graduation. That day, Samuel had been all set to tell her his real feelings—that he was in love with her. He'd had girlfriends in the past, but never told any of them that he loved them. Maggie was the first girl he'd ever truly fallen for. He knew that there would be challenges with them leaving for college, but since they planned to study at the same university he figured there was a chance for them to build a relationship together. When Maggie asked to speak with him privately after the graduation ceremony that day, he thought she might tell him the same thing.

That memory felt so real to him, as if he could still feel the summer sun filtering through the Douglas firs they stood under together. The evening had been hot, and Maggie was wearing a simple white cotton dress that made her pearly skin glow. He could remember the pained expression she had on her face when she looked at him.

As he recalled Maggie's announcement that she was leaving, his gut clenched, just as it had that day. It was a physical pain, hearing that she had decided not to study at the University of Washington, where they'd both been accepted, where they both planned to live on campus.

Instead, Maggie declared she'd decided to attend UCLA instead. Samuel had tried to keep a stoic demeanor, nodding stonily, not trusting himself to speak. Maggie had spoken in a rush, like she'd been holding this news in for a while, and he wondered when she'd actually made the decision to move states.

She'd tried to explain that she needed a fresh start—that everything reminded her of Carlie and she wanted completely new surroundings. As her voice had faltered, she'd looked at him pleadingly, as if begging him to say that it was all fine and he totally understood. But he couldn't do that. He'd merely nodded. He couldn't blame Maggie for her choice. They had made no promises to each other, and they were only friends. She had every right to make the best choice for her future. But that hadn't made it any easier.

He'd considered telling her the truth, but he couldn't stop thinking about her words: *Start fresh*. He was part of what she wanted to escape from. The words *I love you* had died on his lips, replaced instead by *I understand*. He knew Maggie had struggled immensely since the death of her best friend, and he knew how hard it had been for her to be in Vargo, where everything reminded her of happier times with Carlie. He also knew how passionate she was about journalism, and UCLA would be a great choice for her academically.

He knew all of this, and his heart still broke. In that moment, standing on the precipice of their futures, he couldn't burden her with the admission of his feelings. She wanted a fresh start in a brand-new place, and he wasn't going to do anything to hold her back.

"Sam? Earth to Sam?" He blinked and looked up. Maggie was peering at him from across the table in the damp cabin on South Rock Island. He forced himself to lurch forward ten years, back to the present. Maggie's sudden return had stirred up emotions deep within him, a whirlwind of confusion he couldn't quite grasp. He had spent his career controlling his reactions, mastering his own mind, and yet the flood of memories and maelstrom of competing emotions was eroding his carefully constructed resolve.

"Sorry, I spaced out there." Samuel cleared his throat. He saw the way Maggie was looking at him, her eyes questioning and intense, and he had to look away. Suddenly the walkie-talkie burst into life. He'd almost forgotten it was clipped to his pants.

"Boyd, come in. Over."

"Go ahead. Over." Samuel held the walkie-talkie close to his mouth.

"I am going to come out to you now. The storm hasn't reached peak strength yet. Can you meet me down at the boathouse? Over." The voice was faint and crackly, but Samuel could understand it.

"Yeah, we can meet you at the boathouse. What's your ETA? Over," Samuel responded.

"ETA twenty minutes. Over and out." The voice signed off.

"Understood. Over and out." Samuel breathed deeply as he reattached the radio to his pants and turned to Maggie. "We need a plan. Whoever this person is, they'll be expecting Boyd and Thatcher...and they'll be expecting *us* to be tied up and ready for transporting."

"We could hide and ambush the person? They won't be expecting us to be lying in wait for them," Maggie suggested.

"We don't have any weapons, and we're not sure this person is coming alone. What if it's more than one?" Samuel stood up and began pacing, letting ideas bubble to the surface of his mind and dismissing them as unworkable, one by one.

After several moments of silence, he had the beginning of a plan. "We have to lure this person—or persons—out of the bay and up the cliff. If we hide along the rocks, we can steal the boat as soon as they are far enough away."

"But what if it's more than one person, and one of them stays behind in the boat?" Maggie asked.

"I know it's risky, but we have to take action or we're never going to get out of here. I think I should radio whoever is on the other end of this radio and tell them that Thatcher is injured, and they're stranded on the cliff. Hopefully then the person will head straight up the island once they arrive," Samuel mused.

"That's a good idea," Maggie agreed slowly.

"Okay, here goes nothing," Samuel said, taking a deep breath. He pushed down on the button and spoke into the walkie-talkie. "Come in, over."

"Go ahead, over." The voice came through a few seconds later.

"Uh, Thatcher is injured. We are unable to meet at the beach. We need you to come up to the cliffside when you arrive and help me transport Thatcher down. Over." There was silence from the other end, stretching out for what seemed like hours. Samuel began to sweat, sure that he had just given up the game and showed that they weren't Boyd and Thatcher.

"Understood. I will head up cliffside. Provide a landmark so I know where to find you. Over." The voice finally came through, and Samuel breathed a sigh of relief.

"Look for the cabin. We are nearby. Over."

"Ten-four. Over and out." The receiver went dead.

"What if they didn't believe you and now they're suspicious?" Maggie asked nervously.

"That's a chance we'll just have to take," Samuel said grimly. "We're all out of options. Our lives are on the line now. It's time to try and take control of this situation again."

The storm outside matched the maelstrom of feelings raging inside him. Samuel knew that if he miscalculated here, he wasn't just risking his own safety, he was putting Maggie in danger, too. All he could do was pray that he had made the right choice here—and that he wasn't leading them to their demise.

SEVEN

Maggie listened to the rain pounding above their heads. Normally it was a sound that relaxed her, but just now it heightened her anxiety. They needed to make their way back down to the beach in the storm and make it back through the rough seas. A sudden thought struck Maggie.

"What about the men? Thatcher and Boyd—won't they be in danger?"

"They're high enough up in the cave system that they should be safe," Samuel responded.

"I think we should bring them out of the caves," Maggie said, concern building in her chest. "They're restrained in a tunnel with the possibility of high rains and tides rising. I know they're probably safe, but maybe we could bring them somewhere they're more likely to be discovered."

"They'll be safe where they are. The police will send someone to get them when they can." Samuel's voice was flat, but she could see he was loath to do anything to help the men. She wondered again what had happened that forced him to leave the FBI. She was sure his lack of empathy was stemming from a place of hurt. On the other hand, she could see his point of view. Her throat still ached where Thatcher had squeezed his hands around it.

"We could just leave them in the boathouse or somewhere on the path through the cliffs. At least it would be safer than those caves," Maggie said beseechingly.

"Those men attacked you multiple times and have proven themselves willing to take your life," Samuel pointed out. "Plus, we're on a time limit. We need to get down to the beach and find a good hiding place before this person arrives."

"Sam, it's the right thing to do," Maggie said simply. They couldn't leave the two men tied up and stranded in a cave during a violent thunderstorm. Despite years of witnessing some of the darkest corners of humanity in her journalism work, Maggie had managed to keep her empathy intact. She always tried to see the humanity behind the headlines she penned, and she hoped her readers could do the same. Leaving Boyd and Thatcher behind went against her code of ethics, no matter how reprehensibly they'd acted.

"Fine," Samuel said with a sigh. "We'd better go and get them, and then get down to the boathouse." He stood up to follow her to the door. Suddenly she saw something glinting beneath the bench that ran across the wall. She felt drawn toward it, almost like an invisible hand was pointing it out for her.

"Maggie?" Samuel was looking at her curiously.

"Just a minute." Maggie scrambled forward and got down on her hands and knees. Dust and grime coated the ground, and she shuddered as tendrils of cobwebs brushed against her hands. She pulled the glinting object toward her and let out a cry.

"What is it?" Samuel was suddenly crouching next to her.

"This is Carlie's necklace." Maggie's whole being was trembling as she stared at the chain pooled in the palm of her hand. It was tarnished in places from being in a damp place for so long, but when she turned the half heart she could still make out the engravings. *S-T* and *E-N-D* on one side, completing her heart to form the words *BEST FRIEND*. On the other side was the word *MAGGIE*. Tears sprung unbidden from Maggie's eyes, falling onto the necklace she was cradling. "I can't believe it."

Samuel placed a warm hand on her back. Overcome with emotion, Maggie turned her head and buried her face into Samuel's shoulder, allowing him to wrap his arms around her tightly. Despite being stranded on a deserted island in the Pacific Northwest in the midst of a violent storm, she felt completely safe in his arms. Safer than she had in a very long time. She couldn't recall a time she'd let herself be so vulnerable with someone.

She allowed herself to be held until her sobbing abated, then pulled back. With the pads of his thumbs, Samuel wiped away the residual tears. He tilted her chin up and their eyes locked. "Are you sure this is her necklace?" he asked.

Wordlessly, Maggie held up the heart and showed him the word *MAGGIE*, before turning hers over to show him where *CARLIE* had been carved into the back. She matched the two hearts together so it made one.

"It's really her necklace," he whispered, astounded. "I can't believe you spotted it under there!"

"If Carlie drowned, why is her necklace here in this cabin?" Maggie wondered aloud. As she pulled on the chain, the links snapped after such long exposure to the elements. She unclasped her own necklace before sliding Carlie's heart off her broken chain and adding it to her own. When she refastened her chain, both heart halves fell against her skin.

"Good question," Samuel said. "Maybe she visited here on a different day, before she died, and lost her necklace?"

"Wait a minute!" Maggie cried, pulling her wallet out from her back pocket. She slid the photo of Carlie out and stared at it, her eyes wide. The photo cut out under Carlie's shoulders, but clearly nestled in the hollow of her collarbone was the same necklace Maggie had just found. "She was wearing the necklace the morning she died." With trembling fingers, she offered the photo to Samuel.

He took the photo and stared at it, frowning. He looked up and met Maggie's eyes. "You're right," he agreed simply.

"So she was in this cabin the day she died!"

"Or someone with her necklace was." Samuel nodded. They sat in silence for a few seconds before Samuel handed the photo back to Maggie. "We need to get going if we want to have time to get Boyd and Thatcher down to the beach. Let's talk about this back at Vargo. Once we're back on the mainland, I can help arrange a forensics team to do a sweep of this cabin. It's a long shot after all these years, but maybe they'll still be able to find usable evidence."

"Okay," Maggie agreed. She wanted to stay and do a careful search of the cabin in case they'd missed anything, but the storm was only worsening and their small window of escape would quickly close. They grimaced as they slipped back into their cold, damp rain gear and stepped outside.

Maggie began shivering immediately as they dashed through the downpour. Thunder crashed overhead, followed by a celestial whip of lightning. They stayed under the trees as much as possible. Maggie's sneakers slipped and slid on the path, which the rain had turned to mud.

Samuel's sure steps led them to the gap in the cave tunnel. "Stay back!" he yelled over the sound of the pelting rain, and she reluctantly stepped back, trying to gain a little shelter beneath the tree branches surrounding the exposed cave section. She watched nervously as Samuel pressed his back against the exposed section of tunnel, tenting his hand above his eyes to stop the driving rain obscuring his vision. He tentatively stepped inside, and Maggie could feel her heart thumping, terrified, as she waited for him to reemerge.

It felt like an eternity before she saw his long legs step back out of the tunnel.

"They're gone!" he said, holding up the strands of broken rope that before had restrained the two men.

"Where?" Maggie called back, immediately feeling silly. How would Samuel know that? She cast her eyes around them, as if the men were going to jump out of the shadows at any moment. There was nothing but rain all around them, falling in glittering curtains.

"Let's get out of here." Samuel was next to her now, grabbing her elbow. His eyes were constantly flicking side to side and all around, aware of everything around them. There wasn't enough room for them to run side by side down the hill, but Maggie held tight to the back of his jacket and followed him as they ran full speed toward the bay. Several times she stumbled forward, his bracing frame the only thing stopping her from tumbling head over heels down the sodden trail.

Every crack of thunder and flash of lightning made her jump. She was on high alert, expecting at any moment to be tackled to the ground or to hear gunshots ring out. Her head was still pounding where Thatcher had hit her with his weapon. Each throb pumped a wave of nausea through her.

At the point where the trail morphed into a steep fall, Samuel stopped.

"I'll go first and wait at the bottom to make sure there's no one there. Wait for me to wave you down." He had to lean close to her ear and speak loudly for her to hear over the torrential downpour. She caught his familiar scent, a unique blend of warm musk and the spicy notes of his cologne, peppery and sharp. Just as quickly as she noticed, the scent disappeared with Samuel as he disappeared down the path ahead of her.

She crouched beneath a Sitka spruce, holding on to a large rock that enabled her to lean forward. Samuel had disappeared beneath the steep drop that led down to the bay below. She could see the curve of the rocky shore and waves crashing against it. She knew the waves were going to get worse, but they were already intimidatingly large. She thought she could make out a boat heading toward them across the rough water, but as she stood to get a better look, a tremendous force pushed her down on the ground.

The breath was forced out of her lungs and, gasping, she twisted her body around to see Thatcher standing above her, leering at her with a spiteful grin. Dark bruises were already forming beneath his eyes, and his nose was swollen and red. She realized that must have happened yesterday, when she kicked him in the face during the first attack.

"Stay down," he commanded as Maggie tried to struggle upright. He used one muddy boot to kick her shoulders back down on the ground, then leaned in closer. Looming over her, he cracked his knuckles threateningly and pressed the same boot against her chest, pinning her to the ground. He looked toward the bay, and after a moment he gave a thumbs-up to someone.

He roughly hauled Maggie to her feet. Reaching out, he gripped her hair tightly and pulled her face close to his. She could smell his rank breath and see the yellow coffee stains on his teeth as he hissed, "Don't try anything like before—or all bets are off."

She stumbled as he pushed her toward the edge of the cliff. Below, she could see Boyd. She let out a moan as she realized that Boyd was standing over Samuel, who was sprawled, motionless, on the rocky shore.

He first became aware of the sounds of yelling, and then a sharp pain pierced his skull. He had to blink several times to clear his vision and slowly he began processing what was happening.

He was lying on his stomach, sharp rocks pressing into his abdomen. He was looking at the steep hill he had just come down and realized someone had been waiting for him at the bottom. He turned his head to look the other way and saw Boyd and Thatcher standing over him. He tried to move his hands before realizing they'd been restrained somehow. About ten feet away, Maggie was sitting on a large rock, her hands similarly tied behind her back. The rain ran down in thick rivulets.

"Sam!" She gasped when she saw him looking at her.

"Shut up!" Thatcher strode over and shook her roughly.

"Get your hands off her!" Samuel yelled hoarsely. Pain was beating a steady rhythm at the back of his head.

"You're not in any position to be making demands." It was Boyd this time, looking down at Samuel with undisguised anger. His nose was swollen and bruised where Samuel had elbowed him in the cave.

The roar of a boat came into range. Samuel managed to strain his neck and saw a small white motorboat fighting against the waves. Boyd raised a hand to wave at the person in the boat, and they waved back. Samuel realized they knew each other. He saw the walkie-talkie was now refastened to Boyd's pants. Whatever element of surprise they'd had, it was gone. His plan had never been watertight, but it was completely ruined now.

The person in the boat cut the engine and jumped out, pulling the boat up with a crunch to the edge of the shore. As the person turned around, his face came into focus. Samuel gasped.

"Joey!" he roared. Had Joey not realized the men had restrained him and Maggie?

Without responding, Joey motioned them closer. Boyd hauled Samuel to his feet with difficulty, and Thatcher roughly shoved Maggie toward the shoreline. The gears began spinning in Samuel's mind, and an unthinkable truth emerged: Joey had betrayed them. Fury surged through him, hot and unforgiving. The betrayal cut deeper than his physical wounds, merging with shame and guilt as he realized his connection with Joey was the reason they were in this danger. Maggie had been right to distrust the local police, and Samuel's own blindness to this possibility meant they might soon be facing their deaths.

"Took you long enough to get this done," Joey shouted above the rain at Boyd and Thatcher.

"They knocked us out!" Boyd's voice was whiny.

"You're fortunate you got the walkie-talkie back or they could have ambushed me," Joey grumbled. "*And* I had to come save you guys in the middle of a storm. Get in!" Joey's ire was clear. He didn't even look at Samuel or Maggie, just motioned for them all to jump into the boat.

"Joey, why are you doing this?" Samuel yelled. Joey didn't make eye contact, just held firm to the boat and motioned again for them to get in. Boyd pushed Samuel into the waves. He was glad for the protection, however minimal, the gaiters offered against the freezing ocean water.

With his hands tied it was difficult to clamber on

board, but he clumsily threw himself over the edge of the boat into the back of the three rows of seats. Boyd climbed in afterward. Samuel watched anxiously as Thatcher nearly threw Maggie into the middle row. She landed with a loud grunt on the seats.

"Be careful!" Samuel yelled, but none of the attackers even glanced at him. Once Thatcher was sitting next to Maggie, Joey turned the boat around and they sped out into the inlet. Samuel looked around him, hoping desperately to see another boat that he could signal to for help, but no one else was foolish enough to be out in this storm.

Samuel's pulse thundered in his ears, matching the screech of the boat engine. The fury he felt burned through him, and his every instinct was telling him to lash out. If he hadn't been restrained, he didn't know what he would have done. Part of that fury was aimed at himself. If he hadn't been so blind, they might not be in this situation at all.

The waves were treacherously high, the boat slamming against them with tremendous force. Joey made a sharp turn to avoid tipping the boat, and Samuel was thrown down on his side against the seat. Boyd used the opportunity to lean down on him to prevent him sitting up again. With his hands tied, even Boyd's smaller stature could keep Samuel pinned.

Dear Lord, I am calling on You. I am utterly powerless. Please be with Maggie and keep her safe. Please guide my hand to protect her. Samuel felt his prayer bolster his heart, strengthening him for what was to come. He kept his eyes trained on the back of Maggie's head. Centering his attention on her gave him focus and clarity.

He knew he had to protect her and help her finish what she had started. He was going to do whatever it took to help her find out what happened to Carlie. Maybe he was partly to blame for them being in this situation, but he was going to make sure this wasn't the end. They were going to escape.

Eventually the boat began to slow, and Joey brought it to a stop and cut the engine. Boyd hauled him back up into a sitting position, his grin telling Samuel he'd enjoyed his little power trip. It looked like they were back at Vargo, albeit an unpopulated area. Vargo Island wasn't huge—maybe one hundred square miles—but most of the population was concentrated in the downtown area in the southeast. The west and northern parts of the island were largely undeveloped and difficult to access. Samuel suspected they were being taken somewhere in the northwest.

They had pulled up alongside a small jetty, which Joey was tying the boat to. Ahead, a small dirt path led into a heavily wooded area. Thunder boomed overhead, followed by a flash of lightning that illuminated the iron-gray ocean around them. Boyd got out next to Joey, and the two men hauled Samuel out of the boat. Thatcher pushed Maggie ahead of him and held fast to her upper arm.

"Is he waiting?" Boyd asked.

"Yeah, in the cabin. Boyd, go ahead and let him know we're on our way. Thatcher and I will bring these two." Joey gestured to Samuel and Maggie. Boyd nodded and jogged down the path, disappearing into the thicket of trees. Thatcher went ahead with Maggie, and Joey held Samuel's arm.

"Why are you doing this?" Samuel asked again, quietly so Thatcher wouldn't hear.

"I didn't know Boyd and Thatcher were trying to get you and Maggie," Joey whispered, so quiet that Samuel could barely hear him. "Our instructions were to bring in two fugitives."

"Why didn't you say something when you saw it was us on the beach?" Samuel hissed.

"When you get to the cabin you'll understand. I didn't have a choice. Our boss has… He has information about all of us." Joey's expression was pained. "We have to follow instructions."

"They tried to *kill* us. They shot at us. Did you know that?" Samuel couldn't help his voice getting louder. Thatcher looked over his shoulder suspiciously. Once he'd looked away, Samuel said, "We could have died."

"I didn't know about that," Joey said, his voice hesitant.

"My friends have known you for years. I thought I could trust you! How could you betray us like this? We haven't done anything wrong!" Samuel wasn't sure which of his emotions were stronger—fury or disappointment.

"What are you guys talking about?" Thatcher had stopped and was suspiciously regarding them both. He pushed Maggie toward Joey. "You take her. I'll take over the big guy."

"Fine." Joey grabbed Maggie and began walking ahead of them. They strode forward in silence, following the dirt trail through the trees until they emerged at a squat wooden cabin. A tendril of smoke wove through the rain toward the clouds, and warm amber lights glowed in the windows. Tucked against the side of the building was a silver SUV.

Boyd was standing on the front porch next to a short, rotund man. Samuel peered through the curtains of rain, trying to make out who it was. His stomach dropped when he finally recognized him.

It was Police Chief Jones.

EIGHT

Maggie studied the shocked expression on Samuel's face as he gaped up at the men standing on the cabin porch. Boyd stood next to an older man, who leaned nonchalantly against one of the porch railings as though he was merely enjoying the rain without a care in the world. The man's gray hair was parted neatly down one side, his gray button-down shirt tucked tightly into his blue jeans. With a nervous lurch of her stomach, Maggie realized he had a gun holstered to his hip.

"Finally," was the only thing he said before waving them in and going into the cabin himself. She looked confusedly at Samuel but was quickly pushed up the steps, skidding a little on the slick wood. Despite the circumstances, she was immediately grateful for the warmth of the cabin as the front door closed behind her. A large stone fireplace took center stage in the middle of the room, flames crackling in the hearth. She guessed it was getting close to noon, which meant she'd been shivering in her sopping wet poncho for hours.

The older man was standing next to the fire, stretching his hands out in front of him to warm them. Maggie took a moment to scan the room and get her bearings. The single-story cabin was modestly furnished with overstuffed old sofas, an ancient dining set and a basic kitchen. Several closed doors lined one wall, while the other had large picture windows that looked out into a cleared section, though the rain was obscuring much of the view. Taxidermized animal heads hung from nearly every wall, telling Maggie this was a location used for hunting. It also told her they were likely very isolated.

"You were both a real hassle to bring in," the older man said finally, his voice a low growl. He hiked his jeans up and crossed his arms over a generous paunch. His cheeks were bright pink—from a mix of warmth and alcohol, Maggie suspected. If he'd had a beard and a red shirt, he could have passed for a malicious version of Santa Claus.

"Tell me about it," Boyd said, flopping onto a sofa. One searing look from the old man chastened him. He quieted down and stood again, shuffling his feet.

"Do you know who I am?" the man asked, coming to stand closer to Maggie and Samuel. She shook her head, but then Samuel spoke up.

"Jameson Jones, Vargo's chief of police." Maggie's mouth fell open at Samuel's words. Her head swung back and forth between Samuel and the man.

"Very good," Jones chuckled. "And you are Vargo's very own FBI wonder boy, Samuel Reyes. We're honored you've decided to return and grace us with your presence." Sarcasm dripped from each of Jones's words. "Although we haven't had a chance to meet before this, I feel as though I know you both already."

"We haven't done anything wrong!" Maggie blurted out. Jones's gaze swung to Maggie, and she shivered as she stared into his dark eyes.

"I know exactly what you've been doing. Stirring up a ton of trouble, sticking your nose in where it doesn't belong. But that's par for the course for a journalist like you, isn't it, Maggie Dalton?" Jones came to stand inches from her face. His bulldog jowls were quivering slightly with anger, and she could smell stale cigarettes and whiskey on his breath.

"How do you know who I am?" Maggie asked quietly.

"I make it my business to know when I have rats scurrying around my island, messing with the peace and quiet." Jones stepped back. "Boys, why don't you let our guests have a seat? I'd hate for them to be uncomfortable."

Maggie was steered to one of the sofas and sat down heavily. She was leaning awkwardly, straining to right herself while her hands were bound.

"Untie their hands. They're not going anywhere. I assume you patted them down before you brought them here?" Jones raised his eyebrows at Boyd and Thatcher, then groaned when they sheepishly shook their heads. "You two are real dunces, you know? Well, get to it! Search 'em now."

Boyd and Thatcher jumped up, patting down Samuel and Maggie. They removed their phones, wallets and keys before untying their hands. Maggie rubbed her wrists, looking at the scarlet ligature marks blazing across her skin.

"I'm going to take off my poncho," she told Jones. He

shrugged. She pulled it off and spread it out on the seat next to her. At least her sweater and the seat of her pants were relatively dry. Thatcher and Boyd sat across from Maggie, staring at her threateningly. Joey stood next to the single armchair Samuel was seated in.

"You two have made a right mess of things, you know that?" Jones looked at Maggie and Samuel, frowning.

"Surely there's been a misunderstanding. We haven't broken any laws. We are just trying to investigate the death of my best friend, Carlie Rodriguez." Maggie leaned forward pleadingly. "I've been researching her case for months. I got a text—"

"You got a text telling you to come back to Vargo." Jones cut her off. "Who do you think has been contacting you?"

"It was you?" Maggie was blindsided. She felt like she was standing at the edge of a great chasm, staring down into its dizzying depths. Why was the chief of police texting her as an anonymous source? "You? But…how?"

"Anytime someone is poking around on message boards, looking into that death, my team is alerted. There's a real craze now for true crime content, and I'm smart enough to know that a cold case like Carlie's wasn't going to remain quiet forever. It was easy for my team to engage you in a conversation, keep it playing out to see how much you knew." Jones sat down with a grunt on the other empty armchair. "And it was clear to see you knew a lot. Too much."

"So you know that Carlie's death is suspicious?" Samuel spoke up this time. He glowered at Jones, clearly as angry as Maggie was. The chief of police himself knew that her best friend might have been murdered, but instead of investigating further he was trying to silence her. "Why aren't you trying to find out what really happened?"

"Let's just say I have a vested interest in keeping the girl's case firmly closed. There are some powerful people at play here, Maggie, and you are swimming in dangerous waters." He sighed and, for a brief moment, looked exhausted. Maggie saw her chance to get to him, a small chink in his armor.

"I know you want to do the right thing," Maggie said quietly. "Carlie was my best friend. She was smart, and funny, and—"

"Enough!" Jones boomed. "I don't care about some dead girl or whatever vendetta you're on here!"

"Please, Chief, you have the chance to solve this. To bring a family some peace." Samuel's voice was soft when he spoke. "We're both in law enforcement, and I believe you got into it to protect people, to bring justice. Whatever you're doing here, you have a chance to fix it. To make things right."

"'Make things right,'" Jones repeated, then laughed sadly. "That girl chose to stir up a hornet's nest, and she got what was coming to her. That's all you need to know...that's all you're *ever* going to know. There are forces at play here that you have no idea about. I may be chief of police, but I'm nothing compared to the person your friend angered."

"Is that why you tried to kill me?" Maggie asked angrily.

"It's a wonder you're still alive. If Samuel here hadn't

shown up, you would be lying in the woods right now. A victim of a 'hunting accident.'" Jones laughed again, using his fingers to make air quotes. "But we can't be dealing with dead FBI agents, even if they have to run home with their tails tucked between their legs."

"You don't—"

"Zip it, boy." Jones cut Samuel's retort off curtly. "Now we've gotta figure out what to do with the both of you."

"Are you going to kill us?" Maggie asked. She couldn't believe she was asking this question for the second time in one day. She couldn't believe she was asking the question at all.

"Not if we don't have to. We can't just let you go, though, and have you blabber about what happened here. No, we've gotta get a little collateral." Jones rubbed his chin thoughtfully. "I've got my team combing through databases you've never even heard of. Every mistake, every skeleton in your closet, we're going to find out. And once we have enough to know you'll stay quiet, we'll let you go."

"I'm squeaky clean. I'm an FBI agent, remember? You're not going to find anything on me." Samuel's tone wasn't prideful—it was neutral, simply stating a fact.

"But you got a mother, don't you?" Jones's voice was low now, threatening. "And so do you, Maggie. In fact a little birdie tells me your parents moved out to California to be near you? They'll also make good collateral if we need it. And like I said, the people who you angered have power like you wouldn't believe. Just a word, and *pow*!" Jones threw his hands in the air like fireworks. "Your parents can disappear in, say, a gas line explosion."

"You are evil," Maggie hissed.

"Yeah, well, I wasn't always like this. But I've got family, too, Maggie, and I've got a fair few skeletons in my closet. I'd like my grandkids to stay safe and my closet to stay closed. So here we are." Jones motioned to Boyd, Thatcher and Joey. "And these men here are in the same position. They have just as much to lose as me."

Maggie looked over at the men, who all looked serious. She was beginning to understand that this went deeper than she ever could have imagined. Who could Carlie have gotten mixed up with?

Samuel and Maggie were unceremoniously dumped in one of the rooms off the main living space. "Until we figure out just what to do with you both," Jones had stated dismissively. Thatcher handcuffed them and switched on a light before leaving and locking the door behind him. Samuel looked around for a point of escape, but there was nothing—not even a window. He sighed.

Maggie was silent, staring down at the ground. Samuel leaned back and closed his eyes. *Lord, be with me in this moment. I'm scared for Maggie, I'm scared for my family and I'm even scared for my own life. Help me see Your Hand in this experience, and give me the strength to protect Maggie.*

"There's a Bible verse I read at Carlie's funeral, and I've kept thinking about it over the years," Maggie said quietly. Samuel sat up and looked at her as she closed her eyes and began quoting from memory. "'And moreover

I saw under the sun the place of judgment, that wickedness was there. And the place of righteousness, that iniquity was there. I said in mine heart, God shall judge the righteous and the wicked—for there is a time there for every purpose and for every work.'"

"Ecclesiastes 3?" Samuel asked. He had memorized many Bible verses throughout his life, and though he was rusty now, it sprang forth as though he had just read the verse that morning. He was grateful for the spiritual education his mother and grandfather had instilled in him.

"Good memory!" Maggie smiled. "Sometimes it seems like there is so much evil in this world, and I feel this urge to fix everything. This verse reminds me that there is a time for everything, including justice. We just have to be patient sometimes and trust in God's timing."

"Maybe this is the time for Carlie's killers to be held accountable," Samuel replied.

"So do you believe me now?" Maggie asked.

"It was never about believing you, Mags. My FBI training has made me so cynical. I have trouble believing anything unless I'm holding concrete evidence in my hand or I've directly investigated something myself." Samuel watched as Maggie shifted into a more comfortable cross-legged position, her handcuffed hands pulled tightly behind her back.

"Earlier, Jones said that you ran home with your tail between your legs," Maggie said. Samuel felt a wash of hot shame heat his face. "He was wrong. I don't know your circumstances, but I know you. You are honorable and brave, and I know whatever brought you back here wasn't about running away."

"Maybe it was about running away, though," Samuel said quietly. He hadn't really spoken to anyone about the events that led him back to Vargo. He'd shut it all away, figuring if he could just push through he'd be okay. Maggie was the first person he'd even considered opening up to, and he never imagined it would be in a situation like this. "About a year ago, I was working a case with my partner, Dave. We were profiling a killer in downtown Seattle. They'd gone on a shooting spree in the middle of the day and we hadn't tracked them down yet."

"I think I remember reading about that. Some guy that killed innocent pedestrians on a busy street?" Maggie asked.

"Yeah, that's the one. Well, we'd developed a profile for this guy but we still hadn't found any solid leads to arrest him. I got a tip from one of my sources that the killer had been spotted outside a homeless encampment, so I asked Dave to check it out with me." Samuel sighed, the memories of that night fresh and painful. "We found the guy, but he opened fire on us first. He shot me in the leg and hip, and when Dave came to help me, he shot Dave and killed him. I tried to resuscitate him, but his injuries were just too severe. He died on the scene." Samuel paused and took a breath. "I got shot three times. It nearly paralyzed me. I still have a lot of pain in my leg."

Maggie shuffled closer to Samuel. "I'm so sorry, Sam. Did you get the killer?"

"I shot him in the shoulder. He survived, and he's awaiting trial." Samuel couldn't meet Maggie's compassionate gaze. He didn't feel worthy of compassion. "I couldn't live with myself afterward. Dave wasn't just my colleague, he was one of my closest friends. He had a wife and a baby. If I hadn't asked him to come with me, then he would still be alive today." Samuel heard his voice break, and he cleared his throat. "I had three surgeries, and then my grandfather died. He left me his place, and I knew I needed to figure out my next steps. I couldn't go back to the job. I needed time to think and process. Even now, the idea of returning to the FBI fills me with uncertainty. I guess Jones is right—I did run away."

"Sam, look at me." Samuel looked into Maggie's sapphire eyes. "That is *not* running away. You made a choice to give yourself time to heal, physically and emotionally. That takes a lot of courage." She leaned in closer. "Also, Dave's death is tragic, but it is *not* your fault. He knew the risks he was taking in the career he chose. He literally took a bullet for you, and you would have done the same for him if it had been the other way around. The only thing you owe Dave and his family is to live a long, full life to honor them. They wouldn't want you to be ruled by guilt and shame."

For the first time in months, Samuel felt the tension deep within him release a little. A Bible verse blossomed in his mind. "'The thief cometh not, but for to steal, and to kill, and to destroy—I am come that they might have life, and that they might have it more abundantly.'"

"John 10:10," Maggie said, smiling.

"Well, I didn't expect a mini therapy session while being illegally detained," Samuel quipped, making Maggie laugh so hard she snorted. "I've missed your laugh."

"And I've missed you." Maggie was serious now, her

voice low. "I know back in high school we didn't leave things—"

Whatever Maggie was about to divulge was cut short by the locks opening on the door. The door swung open, revealing Joey. He looked worried, casting looks over his shoulder and breathing rapidly.

"You need to run. Now." He crouched and unlocked their handcuffs, letting them fall to the floor. Samuel noticed Joey's hands were trembling.

"You're letting us go?" Maggie asked in a confused voice.

"This is your only chance. Boyd is driving Jones back to the station downtown, and Thatcher is in the bathroom." Joey passed their phones back to them. "Follow the dirt track behind the cabin for about a half mile until it meets the paved road. There's an old shed at the end, and I know Jones keeps a Jeep there. The key is under the visor. Take the Jeep and follow the paved road downtown. There's no cell phone reception out here, but once you get closer to town you should get service again." Joey was ushering them out of the room.

A storm of conflicting emotions crashed through Samuel as he turned and stared at the man who had once betrayed them—now having just risked his own life to pull them from the brink. He wanted to be furious, to hold on to the anger that had kept him steady, but the weight of the moment made it impossible. Gratitude warred with resentment. Disbelief tangled with grudging respect. Finally, Samuel simply said, "Thank you, Joey."

"One more thing," Joey said, waving Samuel's gratitude away with a hand. “I know where the original coroner’s report for Carlie is.”

“I have the coroner’s report,” Maggie said, her face pinched in confusion. “Carlie’s grandfather gave it to me.”

“You only have the amended version of the report. Jones asked me to tie up any loose ends, and I discovered that the file was never destroyed like it was supposed to be. I was going to take care of it, but then all of this happened. Do you know the off-site storage warehouse on the outskirts of town? It’s the big red building next to St. John’s Church?”

“Yes,” Samuel replied.

“The file is in Unit 28. It belongs to the coroner who did the autopsy—Dr. Bailey. He changed the report later but the original one doesn’t list drowning as her cause of death.” Joey pressed a small key into Samuel’s hand. “This will get you into the unit.”

“Thank you for doing the right thing, Joey,” Maggie said sincerely.

“I’m so sorry. To both of you. I really didn’t know it was you they were after. I was never told names.” Joey hung his head, his voice cracking. “I wish I’d never gotten mixed up in all of this. I have gambling debts and… Well, it doesn’t matter. You just need to run. Now.”

Samuel nodded. He grabbed Maggie’s hand and they headed for the door.

“Going somewhere?” They spun around at the voice. From across the room, Thatcher was pointing a gun at them, a thunderous look darkening his face.

“Run, now!” Joey yelled again. He made a dash toward Thatcher. Samuel didn't wait to see what was going to happen. He tightened his grasp on Maggie's hand and pulled her out the front door. They were down the steps and following the dirt track into the trees when he heard a series of shots from behind them.

NINE

The rain continued to fall unabated as they dashed through the trees. Maggie forced herself to keep running despite the gunshots behind them. Samuel helped to propel her forward, his viselike grasp on her hand unfailing.

After a few moments they paused, sheltering beneath the broad boughs of some pine trees. The smell of crushed pine needles and damp earth floated up from beneath their shoes. Maggie wiped the rain from her eyes and wished she'd kept her poncho on. Her clothes were now sodden, a freezing second skin that she attempted to peel away from her limbs.

"Do you think Joey's hurt?" Maggie asked. After his help, she hoped he had gotten away.

"I think he can take care of himself," Samuel responded, casting a concerned look back toward the cabin, which was now hidden behind the thick copse of trees they had wound their way through. "We shouldn't let his actions be in vain, though. We need to get to that Jeep."

"Thatcher might have radioed Boyd that we've escaped." Maggie drew out her phone, hoping wildly that Joey had been wrong about the reception. He hadn't been.

The no-service icon showed clearly in the corner of her screen.

"I'm sure he will, given half a chance," Samuel said. "Even more reason for us to get out of here." They began jogging down the trail again. With each step, Maggie could feel the two hearts bouncing against her sternum. She felt as though Carlie was here alongside her.

It took ten minutes to find the shed Joey had described. It was a rotting three-sided structure, unpainted and unmaintained. Thick tufts of grass grew between the wood slats, and rain splashed off the aluminum sheet that acted as a roof. They approached it carefully, taking the time to gauge whether anyone else was nearby. They couldn't see or hear anything except the intense rain.

She followed Samuel over to the exposed side. As Joey had described, a Jeep was parked inside. It was ancient, with rusted siding and bald tires. Maggie assumed Jones kept it as a hunting vehicle, something that could get him along the wooded trails without worrying about the car being beaten up by potholes or difficult terrain.

The doors were unlocked and they slipped inside, with Samuel behind the wheel and Maggie beside him. The leather car seats were torn and stained and there were no seat belts. Samuel opened the visor and retrieved the key. It took a couple of times for the engine to finally turn over and roar croakily to life.

"Let's hope this will get us to town," Maggie said. She gripped the sides of the decrepit seat as Samuel reversed out and bumped over the grass to the paved road ahead of them. The road was as unmaintained as the shed, littered with holes and wide enough for just one car. Samuel cautiously urged the Jeep forward, the engine emitting squeals of protest.

The rubber on the windshield wipers was coming apart, leaving smears of rain across the windshield. It was difficult to see but Samuel kept the Jeep bouncing along, guiding it around corners and trying to avoid potholes. They continued along the road until it began to even out, the tarmac smoother.

"You know, I'm confused about something," Samuel said, keeping his eyes on the road. "I remember Carlie being super smart, and wasn't she an amazing musician?"

"Yeah, she was a talented guitarist and singer," Maggie said. "Why?"

"I guess I just don't understand what she saw in Shep Todd. I mean, I know the guy was handsome and whatever, but he was also a major jerk. Carlie could have done so much better," Samuel said.

"I agree," Maggie said sadly. She still remembered when Carlie had told her that she and Shep were dating at the beginning of their senior year. She had been shocked and tried to dissuade her friend, telling her she could do a lot better than some loudmouth like Shep Todd. "Honestly, I think she was kind of flattered by Shep's attention. He wasn't a nice guy, but he was still super popular and handsome, and he was very charming."

"That's it? She wanted attention?" Samuel asked.

"Carlie's home life was difficult," Maggie sighed. "Her mom died when she was very young, and her father struggled with drug and alcohol addiction. He was in and out of rehab and she could never rely on him. She was raised by her grandparents. They did their best, but they were both older and tired, and she just never felt like she lived up to their expectations."

"That's so sad," Samuel said.

"Carlie started rebelling in high school. Nothing huge at first, just skipping curfew and not completing her schoolwork, but it got more intense after she started dating Shep. They would skip school and have these huge parties. Plus, Shep was super rich and he bought her things her grandparents just couldn't afford or wouldn't approve of—clothes, jewelry, even alcohol." Maggie unconsciously touched the hearts at her neck. "She was totally enamored by the lifestyle and attention Shep was giving her. Nothing her grandparents said made any difference. Nothing I said made any difference. It was tough."

"It sounds like he was almost brainwashing her," Samuel mused.

"In a way, I think he was. It made our friendship difficult." Maggie paused. "Honestly, the week before she died, we had a huge fight. We were supposed to go see a movie on the mainland, and she ditched me to hang out with Shep instead. I just lost it—I was so tired of being second fiddle to this meathead. We yelled at each other, said terrible things. I regret it every day." Maggie's throat tightened with grief. "The last thing I ever said to her was that I never wanted to see her again. She died a couple of days later."

"She was blessed to have you as a friend. I'm sure she knew how much you cared about her," Samuel said gently. "People say things they don't mean in the heat of the moment. True friendship transcends all of that."

"I suppose," Maggie said. She didn't want to say that one of the reasons she was so fixated on solving Carlie's death was the guilt she felt. She wanted to make it up to Carlie in some way.

Maggie stared out the window at the passing woods. Soon a large red building appeared ahead of them. They were on the outskirts of town, in an industrial area that also housed Vargo's water treatment plant. She had never been to the storage units, but she definitely knew of them. There were summer residents on the island who rented their homes out the rest of the year, and the units were used to store some of their things. Vargo wasn't a large place, and with limited housing many residents chose to utilize the storage sheds, too.

There were no other cars in the parking lot, which didn't surprise Maggie, given the weather. They dashed to the entrance and Maggie read the sign hanging inside. "This is an unstaffed facility. For any emergencies, call the number below." She looked at Samuel. "Guess we're on our own again."

"For now," Samuel responded grimly. "Let's find Unit 28." They walked into the dark interior. Motion sensor lights flickered on, casting a weak glow over the cement floors. Rows of corrugated iron roll-up doors lined both sides of the hallway they found themselves in. Peeling numbers were posted on the wall next to each door. They followed the ascending numbers.

"Twenty-six…twenty-seven…twenty-eight," Maggie counted aloud. They found the door they were looking for. Samuel inserted the key in the simple lock on the handle and, with a screech of protesting metal, rolled the door up. It was pitch-black inside, and it took a moment for Maggie's eyes to adjust. Samuel quickly found a cord hanging from the ceiling and pulled it, bringing a single flickering light bulb to life.

The storage unit was overflowing with detritus. Filing cabinets, old furniture, plastic bins, a clothing rack hung with shirts, paintings stacked and leaning against a wall and many other things that had once lived in Dr. Bailey's house. It was like entering a neglected museum full of the artifacts of a life.

"Is Dr. Bailey still alive?" Maggie asked, tentatively stepping in. Although they'd had the key to unlock it, she felt apprehensive about entering, as though she was intruding.

"Yeah, last I heard," Samuel said, looking around the unit. "He was actually an old friend of my grandfather. A developer built about ten small villas in town a few years ago, and they're used as assisted living facilities for some older people who don't want to leave the island. He's living in one of those. I remember Gramps telling me how mad he was his kids were moving him into an old folks' home. I guess there wasn't enough room for all his stuff."

"No kidding," Maggie responded. She felt claustrophobic in the small, cluttered space. As she stepped forward, dirt and grime crunched softly under her shoes. The overwhelming amount of stuff made it difficult to decide where to even start. "If you were a coroner's report, where would you hide?"

"Filing cabinet?" Samuel suggested. Two hulking beige storage cabinets stood against the back wall. They approached them.

"I'll take this one, you take the other?" Maggie suggested. She pulled the top drawer of hers open, and Samuel did the same for his. The first drawer was stuffed with hanging files containing all sorts of papers—old bills, letters, even some photographs. She rifled through as fast as she could before moving on to the second drawer.

This drawer held more hanging files and bills, but at the back was a shoebox, the lid held closed with a rubber band. She pulled it out, slipped off the band and lifted the lid. Inside were several photographs and a sheaf of papers stapled together. In one of the photos she saw Carlie's face smiling up at her. "I think I've found it!" She held up the box to Samuel.

"Take a look through it. I want to make sure we don't miss anything important here," Samuel said, continuing to rifle through his drawer.

Maggie sat cross-legged on the floor, ignoring the dirt covering the cold concrete. She pulled out the papers first and began reading.

Coroner's Report

Case Number: 2016-18
Name: Carolina "Carlie" Almeida Rodriguez
Date of Death: February 8, 2016
Location: South Rock Island Beach
Age: 18 years

Summary:
On February 8, 2016, at approximately 5:00 p.m., the body of Ms. Rodriguez was discovered by

Mr. Shepherd Todd (age 18) on the beach of South Rock Island. The circumstances surrounding Ms. Rodriguez's death are suspicious, and I recommend a prompt investigation.

Physical Examination:
The deceased is a Hispanic female, 18 years old, who exhibits blunt force trauma to the back of her head consistent with being struck by a solid object. There are visible contusions and lacerations on the scalp, indicating recent trauma. Rigor mortis and livor mortis patterns suggest the time of death occurred within 6 hours of the body being discovered.

Toxicology:
Toxicology samples were collected during the autopsy for analysis. Preliminary results indicate the presence of alcohol in her system, but no other substances were found.

Medical History:
Ms. Rodriguez has a clear medical history with no documented underlying health conditions or medications.

Evidence:
There were no items found near the body that are indicative of having been used in any assault upon Ms. Rodriguez. Whatever item/s were used to cause Ms. Rodriguez's head wounds were not found on or near her person.

Witness Statements:
Initial interviews with witnesses indicate Ms. Rodriguez traveled by boat to South Rock Island with an unknown male subject at approximately noon. There were no reports of a disturbance or sightings of Ms. Rodriguez after this. Mr. Todd, who found the victim, states she left him a message asking him to meet her at the island after school. He states she was deceased when he arrived and his attempts at resuscitation failed. Further interviews are ongoing to gather additional information and identify potential suspects.

Cause of Death:
The cause of death is determined to be blunt force trauma to the head. The manner of death is pending further investigation, including toxicology results and forensic analysis. No water was found in Ms. Rodriguez's lungs, ruling out drowning as cause of death. Homicide is strongly suspected.

Conclusion:
The death of Ms. Rodriguez is being treated as suspicious and potentially homicidal due to the presence of head trauma consistent with blunt force injury. The investigation remains active and ongoing to identify the perpetrator(s) and determine the circumstances leading to her death.

Respectfully submitted,
Dr. Thomas Bailey
Coroner

"Sam," Maggie whispered, shock tightening her throat. "Sam!" she called again, louder.

"What is it?" Samuel came over and knelt next to her, one hand on her knee, looking at the paper in her trembling hands.

"This report lists Carlie's death as suspicious. It says she didn't have any water in her lungs so she couldn't have drowned, and she had blunt force trauma to the back of her head!" She pushed the papers into Samuel's hands and fished out her phone. She noticed there was still no phone reception, but quickly opened her Photos app. She scrolled up and found the scanned images of the report Carlie's grandfather had given her. "These two reports are completely different." She zoomed in and showed Samuel the cause of death section in the scanned report.

"This one says water was found in her lungs and accidental drowning is suspected due to inebriation," Samuel read. "It's been completely altered."

"That's not all!" Maggie cried, anger making her heart pound. "There's no mention of any kind of head trauma, and it reports her as having high levels of alcohol in her system. In her medical history it says she has a history of mental illness, and there are no mentions of witnesses seeing her in a boat with another man!"

"They're victim blaming. They're saying Carlie was mentally ill and drunk, and she somehow drowned and washed up on South Rock Beach," Samuel said slowly.

"Why would the coroner change his report so significantly?" Maggie put her phone away and flicked back through the paper report, hoping it would divulge more secrets. "Carlie was obviously killed, and the coroner is covering it up. *Why?*"

"The report mentioned that Shep Todd found her. Do you think he's capable of murder?" Samuel asked.

"Shep? He was an arrogant jerk in high school, but I don't know if he could kill someone." Maggie thought back to senior year, when Carlie and Shep began dating. He was a handsome jock, so rich his father had bought him a Mercedes-Benz for his seventeenth birthday. He struggled academically but skated on his good looks and money. Shep's father had been some business bigwig with political connections, and soon after Carlie died he moved their whole family out east, where he was later elected as governor, last Maggie heard. Could Shep have killed Carlie and had his father cover it up?

"We have to consider it as a possibility until other evidence is revealed. Statistically, it's much likelier that Carlie was killed by a boyfriend or someone who knew her," Samuel said sadly. He picked up the box at Maggie's feet and studied the photos.

"I forgot there were photos in there," Maggie said, reaching for the box.

"No," Samuel said quickly. He pulled the box away. "Trust me, you don't want to see these."

Samuel stood up, the box in his hand, and withdrew the photos. They were crime scene photos of Carlie, lying prostrate on the South Rock Beach. Dead. He didn't want Maggie to have that image of her best friend in her mind. He knew that, as a crime reporter, she had likely seen her fair share of death, but seeing your friend's lifeless body was a whole other level of trauma. He wanted to protect Maggie from that kind of pain, after his experience watching Dave die.

"What is it?" Maggie asked.

"Crime scene photos," Samuel said shortly. Maggie nodded, understanding his meaning. Tears sprang to her eyes.

"I want to remember Carlie as she was. She was beautiful and vibrant. It's such a tragedy," Maggie said. She wiped tears from her eyes and stood up, dusting off her pants. "Did you find anything in the storage cabinet you were searching?"

"Actually, yes, a couple of things." Samuel put the photos in his back pocket and returned to the cabinet drawer he'd left open. He reached into a hanging file and pulled out two photos in an envelope he'd found. "This might explain what made Dr. Bailey change his original report." He held up the photo for Maggie to see. In it stood the man Samuel knew to be Dr. Bailey in a suit and tie, his arm around the shoulders of a stately gentleman with thick salt-and-pepper hair combed back from his face. They stood next to a bride and groom, obviously at a wedding.

"Who is this?" Maggie asked, staring closely at the photo.

"This is Dr. Bailey," Samuel said, pointing to the man in the suit. "And this is Michael Todd." He pointed at the tall man being embraced by Dr. Bailey.

"Shep's father?" Maggie asked quietly.

"That's the one," Samuel confirmed. He pointed to the bride and groom. "I'm pretty sure the groom here is Dr.

Bailey's eldest grandson on his wedding day. I vaguely remember meeting him when my grandfather would take me fishing with Dr. Bailey."

"So Dr. Bailey knew Shep's father well enough that he invited him to his grandson's wedding." Maggie shook her head. "If Shep killed Carlie, I can totally see his father covering it up. Shep always ran to daddy when he had problems."

"I remember," Samuel said. In high school he'd played on the football team with Shep. Samuel was the starting quarterback, and Shep hated him for it. He tried spreading rumors about Samuel, attempting to malign his character. After that didn't work, Shep tried to get a rise out of Samuel in different ways. One day Samuel came out of school to find his car windshield smashed. It was an old Toyota he'd saved up all summer to buy, and he'd only had it a couple of weeks. School surveillance camera caught Shep smashing the windshield. For any other kid, it would equal a suspension from school and being kicked off the football team. But Shep's dad stepped in. He paid to replace Shep's windshield, made a sizable donation to the school toward the ongoing renovations of the gymnasium and Shep faced no further consequences.

"What else did you find?" Maggie asked.

"A newspaper clipping," Samuel responded. He held it out for Maggie to see. It was taken from the local newspaper after Shep had won a surfing competition. The photo above the text showed Carlie standing between Shep and Michael. Shep was grinning widely, holding a trophy. Carlie, however, had a tense expression on her face. She looked as though she was trying to step away from the group, and after a moment Maggie saw why. Michael was pressed close to Carlie, his arm around her waist possessively. His head was leaning toward her, his mouth curled in a smug smile. "Does this seem strange to you?"

Maggie took the clipping and examined it, biting her lip as she considered it. She tucked a damp stray curl behind her ear in a familiar gesture that almost pulled Samuel back into nostalgic memories. "A little. Why is Michael holding on to Carlie like that?"

"That's what I want to know," Samuel murmured.

"I mean… Carlie was dating Shep. Maybe she and Michael were close?" Maggie suggested.

"I still think it seems off," Samuel responded. It wasn't the pose on its own, but the expression on Michael's face that went with it. Something about the scene aroused Samuel's suspicions. "Did Carlie ever mention anything about Michael?"

"Actually, I do remember her mentioning something," Maggie recalled. "I know there were a few times that she didn't want to go to Shep's house because she thought Michael would be there. When I asked her what the issue was, she wouldn't really tell me anything other than he made her uncomfortable."

"Interesting," Samuel said, taking the clipping back.

"Do you think Michael had feelings for Carlie?" Maggie asked.

"It kind of looks like that," Samuel replied. "At the very least, this photo shows him being overly familiar with her—and she doesn't look thrilled about it."

"So maybe Shep was angry at his father?" Maggie asked.

"I'm wondering if Shep was jealous and got angry at Carlie. Maybe an argument got out of hand and he hit or pushed her hard enough to cause that trauma to her skull," Samuel mused.

"Whatever happened, I do think Shep was mixed up in it," Maggie said. "I wasn't sure before, but after reading Dr. Bailey's reports? It's clear Carlie's death wasn't an accident."

"Exactly. The witness statements in the original report put Maggie in a boat with an unknown male suspect. What if Shep left school earlier than he reported and took Maggie out to South Rock Island in his boat? Remember how easy it was to skip school, especially in senior year?" Samuel tucked the two photos into his back pocket, along with the crime scene photos of Carlie. "I think we need to pay Dr. Bailey a visit. We need to find out what made him decide to change his original report."

"Do you know where he lives?" Maggie asked.

Samuel fished an envelope out of the storage cabinet. "This is addressed to him at Villa 3, Salmon Run Villages—those are the assisted living facilities I told you about," Samuel explained. "We need to get out there and talk to him. Once we have that information, I can send everything we have to my guys at the Bureau and we can begin a proper investigation."

"Can't we just send what we have now?" Maggie asked, impatience gnawing at her insistently.

"These guys will want to help me, but even they need more to work with. They're not going to step into another police jurisdiction and reinvestigate a closed death without some very compelling evidence. What we have is good…but it's not quite enough." Samuel stood up and checked his phone. "Still no reception. We mustn't be close enough to town yet."

They left the unit, rolled down the door and locked it. As they began heading toward the exit, the sound of a car pulling up outside stopped them dead in their tracks.

"Over here," Maggie hissed, waving Samuel to the other end of the storage units where an emergency exit door was located. He dashed after her, wincing at the loud creak the door made when she pushed it open.

Outside the rain fell steadily, immediately dampening their clothes again. Samuel cast around and found several large cinder blocks stacked against the side of the building. He carried them over and wedged them against the door. "If it's Thatcher or Boyd, this is one less exit for them to chase us from."

"Let's run," Maggie said.

"It's too far to run to Dr. Bailey's from here. We need to drive. We can dump Jones's Jeep behind the ferry terminal parking lot. The villas are next door to that." Samuel edged to the corner of the building. A silver SUV was parked outside, the exact same model that Samuel had seen parked outside the cabin before Boyd took Jones back to town. He was here. The back windows were tinted black, but Samuel could see through the front windows that the car was empty. "It's definitely Boyd."

"It looks like he's inside now," Maggie said, peering past Samuel's shoulder.

"We need to barricade the front entrance to give us a

chance to escape. I don't want them knowing where we're going." Samuel handed Maggie the car key. "I want you to run to the Jeep. Turn it on and wait for me."

With a nod, Maggie took off in the rain, dashing toward the Jeep. Samuel found a branch, brought down by the storm, and carried it over to the front doors. Crouching low, he slid the branch between the metal handles protruding from the doors. It wouldn't be enough to hold Boyd for more than a couple of minutes, but it could give them a head start. Behind him, Maggie started the Jeep, the engine rumbling loudly. Samuel ran over and jumped into the front passenger seat. As Maggie began reversing, he saw Boyd run up to the double doors and begin pounding on them furiously.

They had their head start, but was it going to be enough? He braced himself against the car door as Maggie swerved along the road, barely easing off the accelerator. The car engine revved as loudly as his heart. If they couldn't get the answers they needed from Dr. Bailey, then not only were their lives in danger, but so was their chance for finding the truth about Carlie.

TEN

The Jeep was old and crotchety, and Maggie wasn't used to driving a stick anymore. The gears screeched in protest as she struggled to maneuver the clutch and maintain her speed on the narrow roads. Casting a quick glance sideways, she couldn't help but laugh at Samuel's pale face as he clutched his seat for dear life.

"Remind me to drive next time," he joked grimly.

"I've got this. Don't worry," Maggie said, trying to sound confident, just as the gears squealed again. "You just give me directions."

Samuel directed her along serpentine roads that soon began to widen as they entered the outskirts of town. Maggie quickly got her bearings and drove them past the grocery stores, hotels and tourist shops, many of which were still closed for the winter season. This downtown area catered to the summer residents and tourists that flooded the island in the warmer months. Vargo residents knew to get the ferry to the mainland for their bigger shopping trips or face the high tourist-driven prices on the island.

Maggie paused outside the ferry terminal parking lot.

It was largely empty, which made sense because the ferry still wasn't running. All services had been canceled for the day and were expected to resume later in the afternoon as long as the storm had passed.

"Park on the other side of the terminal. It's hidden from the road so if Boyd or Thatcher are looking for the Jeep, it'll be harder to spot." Samuel directed, pointing toward a stretch of unpaved gravel tucked behind a stand of trees. Maggie guided the Jeep into a narrow space between the ferry terminal building and a section of woods. She turned off the ignition and pocketed the key.

"Where are the villas?" she asked Samuel.

"Just on the other side of these trees," he responded, pointing through the woods they had parked next to.

"I've had enough of running through wet forests to last me a lifetime," Maggie grumbled, pulling the hood of her sweatshirt over her hair. Her socks squelched in her sneakers with each step. Grains of sand from the beach were still caught against her skin and it was beginning to chafe. Samuel, on the other hand, looked as though he hadn't given the state of his damp clothes a second thought. She knew years in the FBI had trained him to ignore pain, fatigue and the cold, as if his body was just another obstacle to overcome.

"We're getting close now," Samuel said, smiling at her. His smile was uplifting, and she felt strength steady her limbs. Without his help, she couldn't imagine she would have made it this far. Soon they could have enough evidence to finally get justice for Carlie and her family. Her friend's memory could be at peace.

They walked rapidly through the woods, and Maggie

was grateful that this time there was a paved path running between the trees—no more mud to slip on. She prayed as they walked, summoning one of her favorite Bible verses to mind. *But he knoweth the way that I take: when he hath tried me, I shall come forth as gold.* After years of putting her faith on the back burner, it was edifying to realize she'd never forgotten these verses. She thought about how gold must withstand incredible heat to be purified, but that very heat brings the impurities to the surface to be removed. She felt the same was happening to her through the tests she was facing. *Lord, make me worthy to face Your tests. Help me to draw closer to You.*

It took only a few minutes to get through the woods. On the other side was a row of small villas with an ocean view and neat gardens. They walked along the pavement that ran in front of the fences until they found Villa 3. Wordlessly, they opened the gate and walked up to the front door. Maggie rang the doorbell.

"Hello?" A middle-aged woman opened the door, holding a large backpack.

"Uh…hi. We're looking for Dr. Bailey?" Maggie asked.

"Who's asking?" she said, her tone matter-of-fact but not unkind.

"Dr. Bailey is an old friend of my grandfather who passed away recently. We just wanted to drop in and catch up about a couple of things." Samuel's warm tone and easy smile obviously won the woman over.

"I'm his housekeeper, and I'm just leaving. Head on in. He's sitting in the lounge at the end of the hallway." She opened the door for them to step inside, then walked outside herself, battling to open her umbrella. Samuel closed the door and led the way into the house.

The interior was warm, and Maggie could immediately feel the chill beginning to leave her bones. She felt a pang of guilt about the puddles of rainwater they were pooling on the polished floorboards of the hallway as they walked toward a lounge with a large picture window. Beyond the window, the stormy ocean churned beneath charcoal clouds, waves crashing violently against the shore, their whitecaps flashing like fleeting ghosts beneath the stormy sky.

Sitting in an armchair facing the window was an old man with a checkered blanket tucked over his legs. A buttoned brown cardigan strained against his considerable stomach, upon which he rested his hands. He turned to look at the two of them, his round spectacles giving him an owlish expression.

"Hi, Dr. Bailey? I'm Samuel Reyes, the grandson of—"

"Al Reyes," Dr. Bailey finished. "I remember you, Samuel. You're Al's spitting image."

"Thank you," Samuel said. There was an awkward pause. "Your housekeeper let us in. I was hoping you might have a moment to chat with us?"

"I have nothing but time," Dr. Bailey responded, his tone somewhat melancholy. He turned his gaze to Maggie. "Are you Samuel's wife?"

"Oh! No, I'm not—just a…just a friend," Maggie stammered, blushing. "My name is Maggie Dalton. I used to live in Vargo, but I moved to LA about ten years ago."

"Welcome home," Dr. Bailey said. He waved a hand at the love seat positioned opposite him. "Take a seat."

Maggie settled herself on the sofa with Samuel right next to her. His leg pressed against hers in the small space, sharing a comforting warmth.

"Samuel, I'd heard you were back in town. I was sorry to hear of Al's passing. He was such a wonderful man," Dr. Bailey began. "He was so proud of you—told me all about how you'd been accepted to the FBI and were working as an analyst for them."

"Yes, sir, it's certainly been an adventure," Samuel nodded, pausing before adding, "I miss him every day. He was an incredible person." Maggie was moved by the note of vulnerable grief in his voice.

"I understand loss. My wife died several years ago. Some days, it feels like she just stepped out of the room… and other days, it feels like a lifetime since I last heard her voice." Dr. Bailey paused, clearing his throat before looking up again at Maggie. "And you, Ms. Dalton? Are you also an agent?"

"I'm a journalist, actually," Maggie responded.

"Well, an FBI agent and a journalist turning up unannounced at my home certainly makes for an interesting afternoon," Dr. Bailey said, his tone losing some of its warmth at Maggie's admission. He was beginning to become suspicious of their presence. "Why don't you tell me what brings you here?"

"Well, Dr. Bailey, we're actually here to discuss a case you worked on about ten years ago when you were the coroner." Samuel smiled politely. "Do you remember the death of Carolina Rodriguez? She was also known as Carlie."

The color had drained from Dr. Bailey's face, his mouth agape. He looked as though he had seen a ghost. "Carolina Rodriguez," he repeated in a hoarse whisper.

"So you remember her?" Maggie asked, leaning forward in her seat.

"I—I do," Dr. Bailey said, clearing his throat and regaining his composure. "From what I recall, she drowned and was discovered on South Rock Island."

"That's certainly what it says in the coroner's report Carlie's family has," Samuel agreed. "However, I'm sure you remember that you wrote another version. Your original report is significantly different from the official one that is currently still on file."

"I don't recall another version," Dr. Bailey said unconvincingly.

"Allow us to refresh your memory," Maggie said, pulling the report they'd found at the storage unit from her pocket and handing it to Dr. Bailey. He opened it with shaking hands and skimmed it quickly, his mouth a hard line.

"Where did you get this?" he asked, not taking his eyes from the paper.

"In your storage shed, actually. An acquaintance gave us a key, and we went ahead and took a look," Samuel said.

"But that's breaking and entering! You didn't have my permission to be in there!" Dr. Bailey protested.

"Considering what's in your original report, I don't think you're in a position to be talking about illegalities," Samuel said calmly. "Can you explain why there are such significant variations between the two reports?"

"Variations? Well, new information came to light. I made…adjustments." The old man wasn't meeting their eyes, and his hands were still trembling. Maggie would have felt sorry for him if she wasn't filled with frustration at his obfuscation.

"Listen, you need to—" Maggie began, but Samuel placed a steadying hand on her knee and shook his head. She took a deep breath and began again. "Dr. Bailey, Carlie was my best friend since first grade. I was devastated when she died, and it nearly destroyed her family. We all left Vargo, and a big reason for that was because it reminded us too much of her. We aren't trying to get you in trouble, but we really want to get to the bottom of what happened to Carlie. She deserves justice, and if you have information that can help us, we are begging you to tell us."

Dr. Bailey remained stone-faced, his arms crossed obstinately over his chest. Samuel shifted beside her, then leaned forward and extended his hands, pleading with the doctor to listen to him. "Dr. Bailey, you said earlier that you understand loss, and so do I. We are asking you to think of Carlie's grandparents—the good people who stepped in to raise her when her own parents could not. Imagine if you were left with a false story about the passing of your wife. Imagine if you never got closure for her death. Please, don't do that to someone else."

"You don't understand," Dr. Bailey muttered quietly. He finally met their gazes. "What I wrote in the original report… I should never have kept it. I was supposed to have destroyed all copies. I nearly did! We wiped all the servers clean and replaced it with the version that her family has. I just couldn't bring myself to destroy all the copies and photos. I thought I could keep some of it as collateral, but I guess I'm not as good at keeping secrets as I thought. Someone obviously found out I'd kept some."

"But why did you have to destroy anything?" Samuel asked.

"I'm an old man now," Dr. Bailey said after pausing for a moment. "My life doesn't matter much anymore. But the lives of my children and my grandchildren are at stake. I have to protect them."

"Dr. Bailey, you know I work for the FBI. I promise you, if you help us, I can protect your family. But we can't protect you if we don't know what is going on," Samuel implored.

"*He* probably knows people in the FBI, too," Dr. Bailey said.

"Whoever you're talking about, they aren't so powerful that they've breached all levels of government. I know and trust colleagues in the Bureau. I promise I can protect you and your family. But you have to tell us what you know." Samuel spread his hands open. "We have no ulterior motives in coming here. We only want to find out the truth about what happened to Carlie. So, please, tell us who you're so afraid of." Maggie felt a swell of admiration for Samuel's interviewing skills.

Dr. Bailey looked up with tears in his eyes. "Michael Todd."

* * *

Samuel felt his blood run cold. "Michael Todd? Shep Todd's father?"

"The very one." Dr. Bailey drew in a shaky breath. "You know he's a governor now? And I believe he is going to make a run for president in the near future. I've watched his political career closely, hoping that one day someone might discover the truth about him."

"And what's the truth?" Maggie asked.

"That he's corrupt to the core. He was the one that had me change Carlie's coroner's report. He was the one that tried to have every trace of my original report wiped from the face of the earth." Dr. Bailey was becoming agitated, spittle collecting in the corners of his mouth. "When I issued my original report, he came to my home and threatened me in the middle of the night. Said if I didn't change it I'd be in danger, as well as my family. I didn't believe him, though. I went to speak to the police."

"Chief Jones, by chance?" Samuel asked.

"You've had a run-in with him, I'm guessing?" Dr. Bailey observed them astutely. "You're correct. I tried to report Todd to Chief Jones, and he told me the same thing. Todd has deep pockets, and Chief Jones has been paid off by him. Probably threatened, too, come to think of it. Anyway, the day after I spoke to Chief Jones, someone ran me off the road on my way to work. It's astonishing I survived. I knew he wasn't lying after that."

"So you changed the coroner's report after Todd threatened you?" Maggie asked.

"Yes. I'm not proud of what I did, but I was scared." Dr. Bailey pinched the bridge of his nose as tears fell down his cheeks. "I think of that girl every day. She didn't deserve what happened to her. I wanted so badly to give her family peace. I think that's why I kept some of my own evidence. I thought maybe one day Todd would be found out, and I would be free to share what I knew."

"We found photos in your storage cabinet, too." Samuel pulled out the photos and passed them to Dr. Bailey, who slowly flipped through them. His expression was haunted, memories clouding his eyes like ghosts.

"I remember reviewing these photographs," Dr. Bailey said slowly. "In the report that her family received, the one that's still on record, all you can see is her body and since she's lying on her stomach, there's no way to tell she has any injuries. It was easy to rule her cause of death as an accidental drowning."

"Can you explain your honest opinion about what happened to Carlie?" Maggie asked.

"In a nutshell? She was murdered." Dr. Bailey put the photos on his lap and gazed over his glasses at Maggie. "She had blunt force trauma to the back of her head. You can see the wound in some of the photos—of course, those were not included in the amended report."

"So someone hit her?" Maggie pressed. "Or do you think she fell?"

"It's hard to know with absolute certainty, but my thought is she was hit. Perhaps with a rock or brick," Dr. Bailey said. "If she'd simply fallen, I'd expect to see a more irregular-shaped lesion. The wound to Carlie's head shows a depressed skull fracture. The bone is visibly fractured and pushed inward, suggesting she was struck with considerable force. There are extensive lacerations and tissue damage also."

"So Shep could have fought with her and hit her on the head with a rock or something similar," Maggie said, turning to Samuel. He nodded thoughtfully.

"Shep?" There was a clear note of surprise in Dr. Bailey's voice. "I suppose it's possible, but we had witness statements and school CCTV footage that placed Shep at school until dismissal, at which point he went to South Rock Island and came upon Carlie's body. I always believed he was genuinely shocked to have discovered her."

"You don't think it was Shep?" Samuel asked slowly, rubbing the back of his neck.

"I suppose it could have been. I don't have any alternate suggestions." Dr. Bailey shrugged.

"Why did you keep this clipping?" Samuel asked, holding up the newspaper article about Shep's surf tournament victory.

"I didn't even realize I had that still," Dr. Bailey said, gazing at it. "For a period of time I was trying to do my own surreptitious investigation to see if I could pull together enough evidence to prove Michael Todd had threatened me. I put together a few bits and pieces that showed the timeline of Shep and Carlie's relationship. Just building background information. It was all for nothing, though. I could never find anything solid to help me."

Samuel stood. "You've been very helpful, Doctor. I need to make some phone calls. My reception is still spotty. Do you mind if I use your phone?"

"It's in the kitchen. Go ahead," Dr. Bailey said softly, a grim expression gripping his features.

"We are going to take Michael Todd down before he has a chance to harm you or your family. You have my word," Samuel said, noting the resignation in Dr. Bailey's voice. He shrugged in response.

The kitchen was in the adjoining room—a modern affair of chrome finishes and shiny marble counters. Sitting on the counter was a cord-free landline, and Samuel scooped it up. He used his phone to look up the contact he needed, then dialed the number on the landline.

"Reynolds," came the voice on the other line.

"Jim, it's Reyes," Samuel said.

"Samuel, good to hear from you." Jim Reynolds worked in Samuel's office. They weren't partners, but they had often collaborated on assignments. A few years ago, Jim's partner had been killed on duty, and he was one of the few people who had truly understood what Samuel was going through in the wake of Dave's death.

"Jim, I need a favor," Samuel said.

"Of course."

"This is...time sensitive. Can I get your help and explain everything after?" Samuel asked.

"Sure," Jim said, drawing the word out in uncertainty.

"I'm back in my hometown—Vargo Island, Washington. I'm helping an old friend investigate the death of a high school friend of ours. It had been ruled as an accidental drowning, but we have solid evidence now that she was murdered," Samuel said. "Before you ask, we've tried to investigate this through the usual channels, but—and this is where it gets muddy—there's a whole lot of corruption we're encountering. Turns out our police chief is in the pocket of a pretty powerful man, and it's looking more and more like that powerful man is responsible for covering up the murder."

"Huh," Jim responded in his usual understated manner. "So who is this powerful man?"

"Michael Todd."

"As in… Governor Michael Todd?" Jim said in astonishment.

"Yes. I know this sounds crazy, but I wouldn't call you if I wasn't sure."

"I know you wouldn't. What do you need me to do?" Jim asked.

"Can you run some checks on Todd? I need to know more about his financial history, if he has any known contact with suspicious individuals, if there's been any reports made about him. Anything, really, that I could use to build my case." Samuel paused. "And I need it fast. There are people's lives on the line."

"How fast is 'fast'?" Jim asked. Samuel could already hear him clacking away on his keyboard.

"Can you get it to me in a couple of hours?" Samuel knew it was a big ask. "I have the number of an anonymous source that was contacting a…collaborator of mine. The chief of police admitted the source was his own team, but I need a solid link to that."

"Ha!" Jim's booming laugh came down the phone line. "You don't mess around when you ask for favors. If it was anyone else I'd tell them where to stick it, but for you… I'll do my best. Go ahead and give me that number."

"Thank you, Jim. I really owe you one." Samuel

breathed a sigh of relief, gratitude for his friend making his heart swell. He read out the number Maggie had given him earlier.

"You owe me more than one, buddy," Jim said, still chuckling. His tone suddenly became serious. "Listen, if you're right about all of this, then you need to keep your head down. It sounds like you're dancing with some pretty heavy hitters."

"Will do. Thanks again, Jim. When you get the info, can you just text it to me? My reception is spotty but it looks like I'm getting some service here and there."

"You got it." Jim hung up, and Samuel replaced the phone in its charging cradle. He looked back into the lounge where Maggie and Dr. Bailey were sitting. Samuel rejoined them.

"Who were you speaking to?" Maggie asked as he approached.

"A Bureau buddy. I'm going to try and get some more information on Michael Todd." Samuel checked the time on his phone. It was nearly 1:00 p.m. The last few hours had felt like days, and he registered the exhaustion in his body. It had been a while since he'd run a case as intense as this.

"Do you think we need more evidence? Don't we have enough now, with Dr. Bailey's testimony?" Maggie asked.

"Not to bring down someone like Michael Todd," Samuel replied. He looked at the doctor. "We need your recorded testimony."

"Haven't I given you enough already?" The old man

was becoming agitated, fidgeting at the edges of his blanket with a morose expression on his wrinkled features.

"Once we have this, we'll get out of your hair." Samuel saw the old man was still unsure. "Michael Todd won't see this evidence unless we're sure we have him cornered. By then, it'll be too late for him to exact revenge. He'll spend the rest of his life in a jail cell."

"I need assurances that my family will be protected," Dr. Bailey sighed.

"You have my word. Maggie, can you record this on your phone? I'm going to ask the doctor a few questions." Samuel grabbed a wooden chair from the kitchen and brought it to sit closer to Dr. Bailey. Maggie stood and began filming.

ELEVEN

Maggie uploaded the video recording to the encrypted file-sharing service she used for all her interviews, thankful she finally had a single bar of reception on her phone. She'd photographed and uploaded the other evidence they'd obtained, too.

Dr. Bailey had gone to the restroom. Maggie stood next to Samuel, looking out at the ocean. The rain was beginning to let up, patches of cornflower-blue sky peeking through the iron clouds.

"Will this video be enough?" Maggie asked, pocketing her phone.

"We have the video testimony, the original coroner's report, the missing crime scene photographs, the photo of Carlie showing she was wearing her necklace that day and the necklace we found in the cabin," Samuel recited, holding up a finger for each piece of evidence. "That's a good start, but we need more. My colleague is going to send us anything he finds, but I think we might need a confession."

"A confession?" Maggie laughed bitterly. "Sure, let's

go ahead and ask Shep Todd nicely. I'm sure he'll tell us everything."

"Mags, I know this is frustrating, but this is my job. Even people as corrupt as Michael and Shep Todd deserve a fair trial, and if we try to use the evidence we have I don't think we have a strong enough case." Samuel placed a comforting hand on her shoulder. "I want these men to go to jail for a very, very long time. Let's not leave them any wiggle room."

Maggie sighed. Samuel was right. His calm demeanor and logical reasoning were perfect antidotes for the anger and agitation swirling through her body. She felt gratitude wash away the intensity of her anger, unexpected and overwhelming, tightening her throat. She had spent so long carrying this weight alone, convinced no one else would fight for the truth the way she would—but here he was, steady and unwavering, standing beside her when she needed it most. The thought of facing this without him now felt impossible, and for the first time in a long time, she didn't feel alone. She knew he had her back.

"Dr. Bailey has been gone for a while. I'm going to make sure he's okay," Maggie said, hoping there would be a time soon that she could eloquently express these feelings to him. Samuel nodded, and she headed off in the direction Dr. Bailey had gone. The second hallway led out of the lounge and branched off into a couple of bedrooms and other closed doors, the first of which Maggie assumed was the bathroom. She stood outside and knocked on the door. "Dr. Bailey, are you okay?" She repeated herself when there was no answer.

"You need to get out of here," came the doctor's reedy

voice after Maggie knocked a third time. A feeling of trepidation swept over her.

"What do you mean?" she asked through the door.

"I mean, you need to get out of here if you value your life!"

"I'm coming in, Doctor!" Maggie shouted. She twisted the doorknob, surprised to find it unlocked, and cautiously peered around the door. What she found wasn't a bathroom, but a small office. Bookcases lined one wall and an impressive mahogany desk stood against the opposite wall. Behind the desk, Dr. Bailey sat at a leather chair, replacing the receiver of an old-fashioned desk phone in its cradle. Maggie's stomach dropped. "What have you done?" she asked in dread.

"I had to," Dr. Bailey said, looking at her mournfully. "I know Samuel thinks he can keep my family safe, but they'll find a way to get to me before they can be arrested."

"Who did you call?" Maggie asked, her voice growing louder with panic.

"I called Jones. He'll be here any minute. He had just arrived at the ferry terminal to keep an eye out in case either of you turned up when ferry services to the mainland resumed." Dr. Bailey spread his hands wide apologetically. "It's nothing personal. I need to keep my family safe."

"You're a coward," Maggie spat angrily. She spun around wildly, shouting, "Samuel!" The silence from the other room sent a dagger of icy fear through her heart. "Samuel!" she shouted again, dashing back into the hallway.

She had made it halfway down the hall when Samuel came racing up to meet her.

"There's someone outside." He appeared calm despite the threat, but Maggie knew he was perturbed. His eyes didn't stop moving, taking in every atom of their surroundings.

"It's probably Jones and Boyd. I just found Dr. Bailey. He wasn't using the bathroom. He was calling Jones. He said he had to protect his family." Maggie's explanation tumbled out in a jumbled mess, interspersed with rapid breaths. She felt like a gazelle cornered by a hungry lion.

"*Unbelievable*," Samuel hissed. "Okay, new plan. Let's go out the back. Jones thinks we're still unaware of his arrival, so we have the element of surprise."

"Where are we going to run to?" Maggie asked, following Samuel to the last door at the end of the hallway. He led them into the actual bathroom, a well-appointed marble affair complete with a soaker tub and large shower.

"Let's get back into the woods. We need to avoid town. I don't know who else Jones is working with. If we can just buy ourselves a little time, my colleague will get back to me with some more information we can use." Samuel pushed at the casement window next to the vanity. "The storm will let up soon, and maybe ferry service will be reestablished. We can head back to the mainland and go straight to the nearest Bureau field office."

"But they're monitoring the ferry service. How will we get on board without them noticing?" Maggie pointed out.

"Let's cross that bridge when we get to it," Samuel replied grimly.

Maggie was conflicted as she clambered out the window, dropping down into ankle-deep mud in the garden bed below. She knew they were in danger as long as they remained on Vargo Island, but she didn't want to leave until they had a game plan for tracking down Michael and Shep Todd and getting the confession they needed. Without that, all of their hard work might be for nothing. *First things first*, she told herself, *find a safe place to hunker down.* When putting together big news articles, it had always helped her feel less overwhelmed to break her ultimate goal down into manageable steps. In this case, safety was their first step.

Samuel landed beside her with a wet *thunk*, splattering damp soil up against their pants. She could feel the damp beginning to seep back into her skin after the brief reprieve from the cold in Dr. Bailey's house.

"Stop right there!" The shouted command drowned out the rest of Samuel's sentence. Boyd was racing around the corner of the town houses. He was still over fifty feet behind them, and Maggie felt Samuel push her away.

"Get away from here," he ordered, pointing at the thick woods growing behind the town houses. "Stay in the woods and keep your phone on. I'll call you and find you!"

"What are you going to do?" Maggie yelled, staggering backward as Boyd raced toward them. Samuel simply pointed at the trees again before turning and running in Boyd's direction.

Maggie turned and sprinted to the tree line. Pausing behind an oversize Sitka spruce, she watched Samuel run full force into Boyd. He had the size advantage and was easily able to tackle the slender man around his knees, bringing him crashing to the ground. For a half second she considered running to aid Samuel, but knew she couldn't offer any real physical help. She clambered up a small hill and ran without stopping, emotions vacillating between guilt for leaving Samuel and determination to keep going in her quest for justice. Ultimately, she figured, Samuel wouldn't have sent her away into the woods if he didn't know what he was doing.

After a while she guessed that she was deep enough in the woods to deter any followers. The rain had slowed considerably, but it was still enough to send icy shivers up and down her body. She eyed an ancient pine whose tangled roots had grown aboveground, creating a natural nook in the ground. It was just large enough for her to tuck her trembling body into, providing a respite from the wet weather.

She plucked her phone from her pocket and looked at it, breathing a sigh of relief to see the bars denoting increased reception. She'd forgotten how isolated Vargo was—she was never out of phone reception in LA. She logged back into her secure file-sharing service and scanned the documents and video she'd uploaded. It was a solid start.

But it wasn't enough.

A confession, Maggie thought hopelessly. How on earth would they ever get a taped confession from Shep Todd? It seemed impossible. He may not be the sharpest tool in the shed, but he was probably savvy enough to avoid being entrapped like that. There was no way they would convince him to confess to murder. She looked back through the files again.

"Do we have any leverage to get him to confess?" Maggie muttered aloud to herself. The evidence they had was good, but it wasn't enough. Shep would have world-class lawyers at his fingertips, and she and Samuel would be shut down before they even started.

She was about to put her phone back in her pocket when a sharp chirp erupted from it, signaling an incoming text. It was from an unknown phone number, and Maggie curiously tapped the Messages app to open it. There was no text in the window that popped up, just a video attachment. She opened it and immediately felt nauseous.

The video showed Samuel, his head bowed and hands bound by handcuffs, sitting in the back of a car. The only sound in the video was rain beating against the car roof, a steady rhythm that sounded like a threatening war drumbeat as she gazed at the screen. The video perspective changed, swinging around until Boyd's own bruised countenance filled the screen. Fury blazed in his oily brown eyes. "Get yourself to Jones's cabin. You have one hour until your pretty boyfriend really begins to hurt." The screen went black.

Maggie let the phone drop into her lap before covering her face with her hands. She let tears flood down her cheeks, deep sobs racking her body until her lungs ached. Guilt for leaving Samuel crashed over her like a tsunami. If she'd stayed, could she have prevented this? If anything happened to him, she'd never forgive herself.

In between the wrenching guilt and terror, a warmth

blossomed like a tulip sprouting from a winter garden. *I love him*, she thought to herself. She truly loved Samuel, probably always had. She had spent years running away from situations that required her to be vulnerable because she never wanted to be hurt again the way Carlie's death had hurt her. It had only taken one day for Samuel to break those boundaries down and make her realize that life was short and so precious. He probably had a girlfriend, but she was still moved by the need to tell him her true feelings, whatever the outcome.

She was filled with renewed strength as the desire to tell him moved through her. "Lord, inspire my heart. Please allow me the chance to tell Samuel my feelings. Help me make amends and guide my journey to justice." Without realizing it, she was praying aloud, her words resounding in the quiet woods.

As she stood, a thought tumbled to the forefront of her mind—she knew exactly how she was going to catch these men out.

Samuel groaned as Boyd grabbed him by the collar and roughly pulled him out of Jones's silver SUV. The old police chief jumped out of the front seat and led them up the steps to the cabin, barely glancing at his bloodied quarry. Boyd pushed Samuel ahead of him through the front door, letting it slam behind them. Inside he could see Thatcher sitting in one of the armchairs, holding an ice pack against his head and sporting a bloodied bandage around his upper right arm.

"You only got one?" Thatcher asked, wincing as he adjusted his injured arm.

"No thanks to you," Boyd muttered bitterly. Thatcher rolled his eyes.

"It's not my fault Joey turned out to be a traitor," Thatcher shot back.

"Shut up, both of you," Jones snapped. He sat down heavily, pulling a silver flask from his front breast pocket and drinking from it deeply. He sighed afterward. "What a mess we have on our hands. Where did you put Officer Bartlett?"

"He's handcuffed and stuck in a bedroom," Thatcher responded with a dismissive flick of his hand toward the locked doors lining the wall.

"Did you hurt him?" Samuel asked, trying to keep his voice calm.

"More than he hurt me," Thatcher responded, glaring at Samuel. "But he's still alive, if that's what you're wondering."

"Boyd, put Mr. Reyes away and give me the keys this time. I don't want any chance of him escaping before the meeting." Jones pointed at the same room where Samuel had been detained last time.

"What meeting?" Samuel asked as Boyd shoved him toward the room. Jones didn't answer, instead tiredly swigging from his flask again.

Inside the room, Boyd kicked the back of Samuel's knees, collapsing his legs. Samuel fell to the floor heavily, and before he could turn over Boyd had left, locking the door firmly behind him. Samuel stayed on the floor, his hands handcuffed in front of him, the cold wood soothing his aching head for a moment.

After Maggie had run into the woods, Samuel had

knocked Boyd to the ground, his pistol spinning away from him. Samuel had grappled with Boyd in the damp grass, managing to pin him to the ground and squeeze his arms against his body. He yelled over and over into Boyd's furious face, demanding answers for who killed Carlie.

Boyd, to his credit, had refused to tell Samuel anything. It wasn't until Samuel had struck Boyd's brachial plexus with a swift motion, born of years of training, that the man had emitted a scream of pain. He then admitted that Chief Jones had told Shep and Michael Todd what was going on, and both men were flying in via helicopter as they spoke, despite the weather.

Samuel had thought hard about this admission, his heart and thoughts racing. Would he be able to just walk up and request a meeting with the Todds? He dismissed the idea, using all his FBI training to craft a spur-of-the-moment plan.

He knew Michael and Shep Todd were powerful. They had charismatic and grandiose personalities, with strong senses of entitlement and the need for admiration. They were both highly manipulative and Michael in particular was skilled at portraying himself in a favorable light. He showed an ability to manipulate public perception, and the events surrounding Carlie's death revealed a willingness to prioritize self-preservation above ethical or legal boundaries. He suspected they had a pattern beyond that of exploiting and threatening others to get what they needed, and obviously disregarded laws and rules to achieve their goals.

Samuel suspected Michael Todd, and maybe Shep as

well, had a lack of empathy and a propensity for narcissistic rage when threatened. He couldn't count on appealing to their higher natures. These men were powerful, and they needed to believe they were in control if Samuel had any chance of getting information out of them. He would need to be presented to them as a prisoner—catching them off guard—and see what information they spilled.

Samuel had then stood and then pretended to trip and fall backward. As he did, he grabbed his phone from his pocket, then tucked himself onto his side, as if he were struggling to stand up. He could hear Boyd curse and struggle to his feet before the weight of the man bore down on him. Samuel just had time to surreptitiously tuck his phone into the bottom of his shoe, under his sock, before Boyd struck him hard in the face.

Samuel looked up at the dark roof above him. It must be midafternoon now, and his stomach was rumbling. He hadn't eaten all day, and he was ravenously hungry. He took a breath and focused on his plan. He would need all his wits to pull this off.

He maneuvered into a seated position against the back wall, keeping one eye on the door in case any of them came back. He'd been patted down for a phone before being thrown in Jones's car, but they'd missed his hiding place. He pulled the phone out now, making sure it was on silent.

There was no reception, but Samuel felt a leap of joy to see that some texts had managed to come through before he lost service on his way back to the cabin. He clicked on the first message, his fingers clumsy with the handcuffs on, and saw they were from Jim.

Hey Samuel. Started digging & found out Todd was investigated b4 for campaign finance issues—hush $$? Case got closed but no reason why. He's got big connections. Took screenshots of some docs but didn't download anything—don't wanna raise flags. Did u know his son has a record? DUIs, drug charges, etc.—but nothing has stuck. He hasn't served time. Also I traced that # u gave me, but it's a burner phone—no records. Hope the pics help. LMK what else u need. -Jim

Samuel eagerly opened the next text, which had a series of screenshots in it. There were a variety of different documents that Jim had sent through, including bank statements with certain large withdrawals highlighted, misleading expense reports, memos with cryptic messaging about payoffs and compliance reports that detailed discrepancies between campaign finance reports filed with regulatory authorities and internal accounting records. He also saw multiple police records detailing Shep's run-ins with the law. Samuel scanned it all quickly, knowing he likely didn't have time to dive into it in depth right now, but getting the general gist.

Michael Todd and his son were both crooks, but the investigations that had been started on them had been shut down in their infancy. Most of the documents Jim sent were from the middle of last year, when Michael Todd's presidential campaign was just getting started. The governor had obviously managed to pull some strings—or make some threats—to get the investigations to disappear. Both for him and his son.

This time would be different, though. This time, Samuel had a secret weapon. He had Maggie. There was no way she was going to let Carlie's murderers escape from justice, and he would do everything in his power to help her. She would tell the whole world about this, and she had the platform to do it.

Despite the desperate situation, Samuel smiled as he thought of Maggie. After all these years, his feelings burned just as brightly. He'd managed to cover them well, but it was impossible to hide from how he truly felt. He loved her, deeply and truly. As a teenager he hadn't had the courage to say what he needed to say, but if he'd learned anything this past year, it was that life was unpredictable. He thought of the joke his grandfather always used to say—if you want to make God laugh, tell Him your plans.

Samuel became aware of the sound of rotor blades whirring above him, and he knew the Todds' helicopter was coming in. The sound increased before stopping, presumably landing somewhere nearby. They would be here any moment.

Lord, I pray for Your aid at this moment. Please light the path to justice and truth and help me to follow Your ever-present guidance. Keep Maggie safe, and I beg for You to give me a chance to tell her how I truly feel.

He looked up as he heard footsteps outside the door. Quickly, he turned on his voice recording app, a specialized program that uploaded recordings in real time to a secure cloud database. Without reception the file would only be stored on his phone, but he hoped that if they found it they'd think it had already been uploaded, and as soon as he got back into an area with reception, the recording would immediately start uploading.

He tucked his phone into his belt, praying they wouldn't bother patting him down a second time. As the door locks began to turn, he quickly straightened his legs and sat upright, trying to keep his face blank. The door finally swung open and Thatcher stood before him, a malicious grin scarring his face.

"Well, now, *Agent* Reyes," Thatcher sneered, sarcasm dripping off the word *Agent*. "We request the pleasure of your company at this time. Come with me."

He pulled Samuel up and pushed him back into the main room. It was empty.

"Where is everyone?" Samuel asked, stumbling slightly as Thatcher shoved him forward, forcing him to sit in an armchair.

"You'll see," Thatcher responded, winking malevolently. They waited in silence for a few moments until the cabin door swung open, Jones leading in two men, closely followed by Boyd, who was hovering behind them with two umbrellas like a butler.

The men strode in and looked around, unsmiling.

"As rustic as I remember," one of the men said. Samuel recognized him from the photographs—Michael Todd. The other man motioned toward the fireplace, where warm flames were flickering invitingly. They walked over together and turned around, their backs to the hearth.

The younger of the men looked sharply at Samuel. It

was Shep Todd, his face an older reflection of the high schooler Samuel remembered. He was about to say so but his breath caught in his throat as the door swung open again, revealing the last person he expected to see. His pulse pounded, his mind racing to make sense of what his eyes were seeing.

TWELVE

Maggie stood in the doorway of the cabin, her heart pounding so loudly she was sure everyone could hear it. All eyes were locked on her, and she felt suddenly self-conscious. Would her plan work, or was she about to walk into her doom?

She focused on Samuel, sitting handcuffed in an armchair, and saw the color drain from his face when he saw her. "No," he croaked. She wished she could tell him not to worry, that she had a plan, but all she could do was smile reassuringly.

"It's a party now!" Thatcher guffawed, striding up to her. He grabbed her by an elbow and she allowed him to steer her to a couch adjacent to Samuel. "You just decided to stroll on up here? Well, that saves us a whole lot of time and trouble!"

"You aren't as smart as I thought you were," Jones said, shaking his head. He approached her with handcuffs until a commanding voice rang out from near the fireplace.

"Chief Jones, don't handcuff Ms. Dalton. I want this to be a civil conversation. And please remove Agent Reyes's cuffs. I'm sure neither of them are planning to run again."

As Jones removed Samuel's cuffs, Maggie looked at the men standing by the fireplace.

Michael and Shep Todd.

The years had been kind to Shep, much to Maggie's chagrin. His chestnut hair was swept back from his tanned face in shiny waves. He wore a snug navy suit, obviously made-to-measure judging by the way it fit his broad shoulders and trim waist. Despite the mud outside, his tan loafers had somehow managed to remain spotless.

"Maggie Dalton. Long time no see," Shep crooned, his smile oozing insincerity.

"Yes, what a treat to catch up with some of my son's old classmates. And that's how I'd like us to think about this. A catch-up." Michael Todd strode over to the sofa opposite Maggie and took a seat. Like his son, he was tall, trim and meticulously dressed in a charcoal suit with a scarlet tie. His salt-and-pepper hair was cut short and styled neatly. His silver-blue eyes surveyed Maggie with cold calculation. "I do wish this *catch-up* wasn't happening under such difficult circumstances."

"Difficult circumstances of your son's making," Maggie snapped. Shep came to sit next to his father, and they exchanged glances.

"I would disagree, Ms. Dalton," Michael responded slowly. "There was no difficulty until you started poking your nose into places it shouldn't be. Do you know how much work it's been to try and clean up after you? You should have let sleeping dogs lie."

"Except those dogs were never really sleeping—not for Carlie's family and certainly not for me." Maggie felt the grip of grief tighten around her throat, threatening to overwhelm her. She took a deep breath and reminded herself of what was important here. She needed to stay focused.

"Listen, Maggie, this is a tricky situation for us." Shep smiled, attempting to appear disarming. She could see that he had inherited the same charisma and charm as his father. It didn't work on her, however. The sight of his perfect white teeth in his forced smile turned Maggie's stomach. "What happened to Carlie was unfortunate. I mean, we were dating! I'm sure you can imagine how very devastating it was for me. But her death was ruled an accident."

"You and I both know it wasn't an accident. Someone killed Carlie." She eyed him steadily as she said it, and noted color draining from his face.

"No, it was ruled as a drowning, remember?" Shep said.

"Of course I remember. It's not something you forget easily—your best friend dying under mysterious circumstances," Maggie snapped back. "There's no way Carlie drowned. The official coroner's report—the one that was amended, the one that has been hidden away all these years—rules her cause of death as murder."

"Murder?" Shep whispered in the silence that grew around them. Michael Todd was fidgeting, his feet tapping on the ground and his hands gripping his knees. Shep, on the other hand, seemed to have gone slack, his mouth agape and eyes squinting. "But…but who would have a reason to murder Carlie?"

"I believe *you* murdered Carlie, Shep," Maggie hissed.

"This is an Oscar-worthy performance from you, though. Maybe you should have gone into acting."

"Me? Murder her?" Shep sounded incredulous, his mouth opening and closing like a fish out of water. He appeared sincere, but she wasn't willing to buy his act. She looked to Samuel for support, but he was observing both men with appraising eyes. Shep continued, "I had nothing to do with Carlie's death. Obviously I found her body, and it was very traumatizing, but I didn't kill her. Your accusation is incredibly offensive."

"If you didn't kill Carlie, why have you spent so much time and energy tracking me down? Your goons shot at me! I could have been killed!" Maggie cried indignantly.

"Shot at you?" Confusion clouded Shep's face. "I don't know anything about that. We've been tracking you down all this time because we need you to understand the truth. I had nothing to do with Carlie's death. Her death was an accident."

"If it was an accident, why not let Maggie investigate?" Samuel spoke up this time, his voice kept carefully neutral.

"She's a journalist!" Shep was beginning to get impatient, his voice growing louder. Maggie was reminded of the loud bravado that had been Shep's persona in high school. Everything in life had always come easy to him, the world seemingly designed to cater to him. When things didn't go his way, or when he had to spend any amount of time explaining his reasons for wanting something, he grew loud and impatient. "My father is beginning a presidential campaign, and any bad press could affect his chances of winning."

"That's the only reason you've been tracking me down?" Maggie asked.

"I swear," Shep said, his hand over his heart. "Right, Dad?"

Michael Todd had been looking at Maggie, lost in thought, but he started when Shep addressed him. He was silent a moment longer and then leaned forward.

"This has all been a terrible misunderstanding. I'm sure we can come to an agreement." Michael spread his hands out; a winsome smile that didn't quite reach his eyes stretched across his handsome face.

"Why did you need to come here, Governor Todd?" Samuel asked.

"Why?" Michael asked. "I believe my son just explained why."

"But if this is all just a misunderstanding, why did you need to helicopter in? Why not leave it to some of your staff to come and speak to us? Or even just Shep?" Samuel's voice was still neutral, but he looked to Maggie like a hound who had just picked up on the scent of a fox. "I mean, if you're running a presidential campaign, you must be incredibly busy."

A silence enveloped the room. It pressed on Maggie's ears as she saw color rising up Michael's throat and warming his cheeks, and Maggie could see he was struggling to contain his emotions. Her focus sharpened as her adrenaline surged, quickening her heart rate and heightening her senses. She knew she was on the precipice of learning the truth, listening to the whispers of something important that she hadn't seen before. All her journalistic instincts told her she needed to keep pushing.

"Governor Todd, I can understand why you would be concerned about a journalist printing a story you say is incorrect. Do me a favor, though, and expand on that. Like Samuel said, why couldn't you have your press secretary reach out and organize a meeting with me or my editor?" Maggie waited until he opened his mouth to respond, then spoke over him, a tactic she often employed when interviewing reluctant individuals. "We have been shot at, illegally detained and physically assaulted by men who claim to be working for you. Besides this, we have files and files of information on you and your son that would indicate illicit activities."

"Illicit activities," Michael repeated, tapping his fingertips together. He gazed steadily at Maggie, then at Samuel. "You're both very clever. Would you do me the favor of telling me what these files are, exactly?"

"The original coroner's report, plus Dr. Bailey's filmed testimony that you forced him to change the report under threat of death," Maggie said.

"Hmm, interesting. An adapted—some would say corrected—coroner's report and the filmed testimony of an elderly man, forced to move into an assisted living facility by his children because he cannot be trusted to live alone." Michael began to smile confidently. "I hope, for both your sakes, that's not the only evidence you have."

"We also have missing crime scene photographs and evidence that Carlie was wearing a necklace the day she died which was missing from her body. We discovered it on South Rock Island," Maggie continued. She touched the hearts that lay around her neck.

"The best friend's necklace," Shep murmured, amazed.

He stared at her. “How did you get that? She never took the thing off. I even bought her a Tiffany locket once and she made me return it. She said yours was the only necklace she’d wear.”

“I was hoping you could help us answer that,” Maggie responded, looking pointedly at Shep, who still maintained an expression of bewilderment.

“Oh, please, this can all be ascribed to the faulty memory and poor work habits of an old man and incompetent police force,” Michael said, waving his hand as if to shoo away her words like annoying mosquitoes. “None of this points to my son’s involvement in any way.” Maggie’s hands were trembling, and she balled them into fists. She could see how charming the governor was, how easy it was for him to talk his way out of trouble. This was why Shep never faced consequences in school.

“You know, I agree, Governor Todd,” Samuel said. Maggie looked at him in surprise. “But we also have some very interesting documents that lead us to believe your family may have been engaged in some illicit activities. I have bank statements, expense reports, internal memos and compliance report discrepancies. Tell me, Governor, do you make a habit of paying hush money bribes?” The look of utter shock on Michael Todd’s face reflected the surprise that lurched inside Maggie—making her want to laugh in delight. She could almost taste victory.

Samuel felt adrenaline rush through his veins, pins and needles tingling in his fingertips, his mind focusing to a razor-sharp point. This was what he loved most about his job, the moment when his adversaries were beginning to realize just how much trouble they were in. He could see that Michael Todd had been caught off guard.

"Well, you've done your research." He crossed his legs and leaned back in the chair, attempting to project a sense of ease. "The trouble is, absolutely none of those things points to my son being involved in this. You may have some financial records, but that doesn't indicate murder."

"Oh, I don't believe your son is involved," Samuel said placidly.

"You don't?" Michael and Maggie asked at the same time.

"No, I don't," Samuel said. "Initially I suspected Shep, but then I began thinking about the profile of this crime. You see, Carlie was likely murdered in, or at least present in, the hunter's cabin on South Rock Island the day she died. That's where we discovered her necklace, flung into the far corner. The police had never searched the cabin because her death was ruled an accidental drowning. But why would Shep bring Carlie all the way to the hunter's cabin? Maybe her murder was premeditated, but it seems far more likely that it was an act of passion, or the assailant would have chosen a more inconspicuous way to kill her.

"So, I came to the realization that Carlie was killed by someone she knew, but not Shep. We have witnesses placing Shep at school until dismissal, and we also have witnesses who saw Carlie going to South Rock in a boat with an older male." Samuel paused, studying Michael's face, which had gone deathly pale. "We also know that Carlie left Shep a note, telling him to meet her at South Rock Island after school. Now, why would she do that?

Perhaps because she had a bad feeling about this trip she was taking, but she trusted the person she was going with enough to ignore her instincts. Maybe she left Shep a note because she wanted someone to come find her if anything went wrong."

He could sense Maggie shifting beside him, shock radiating off her palpably. It took all his willpower to keep his eyes fixed on Michael, instead of turning to Maggie.

"Sam," Maggie whispered. "Are you saying…?" She trailed off, seemingly unable to finish her thought.

"I am saying that I believe it was you, Michael, who murdered Carlie." Samuel kept his expression nonchalant, as though he was discussing the weather, even as adrenaline rose up in him like bubbles in a shaken soda.

"Dad?" Shep laughed loudly, looking around at the silent room as if appealing for reason. "Come on, that's ridiculous! Why would my father kill Carlie?" Chief Jones looked at his shoes, shaking his head slightly. Boyd and Thatcher also avoided eye contact, while Maggie looked as if she'd found buried treasure.

"You'll have to ask him that question, Shep," Samuel said.

"This is ridiculous. Dad?" Shep swallowed visibly when his father wouldn't look at him. "Dad, tell them it's not true!"

"Yes, Governor Todd, tell us," Samuel said icily. "Or perhaps I'll leave it to my colleagues at the FBI. They already have all of the evidence I mentioned, and there is more than enough to bring either one of you in. Considering Shep has multiple police records already, I'd say he's going to be the favorite when the police investigate this. And it is a *when*, Governor, not *if.* You might be able to cover up financial crimes and clean up Shep's DUIs and drug charges...but murder is a whole different ball game."

"Dad...please... I didn't... I didn't do this!" Shep was stammering, his pale, terrified face like a ghost caught in a moonbeam, drained of all warmth and color. Samuel noticed with some satisfaction that Shep's hands were trembling.

"Shep, stay quiet. Pull yourself together," Michael hissed at his son in disgust. Shep ignored him.

"Dad, you've got to help me. I swear on my life—I had nothing to do with Carlie's death!" He was crying now, and Michael Todd looked away from his son, shaking his head. Shep's shoulders heaved with each ragged breath, sobs tumbling from his lips like a child lost in the dark. His eyes, wide and glistening, brimmed with terror. He reached out and grasped his father's arm. "Dad, you have to believe me! I'm your son, I swear I wouldn't lie to you!"

"I know that! I know that, Shep!" Michael finally exploded. He pulled himself away from his son, and moved to stand behind the couch. He leaned forward, both hands braced against the back of the couch as if for support. Strands of his hair had come loose and his cheeks were burning with emotion.

"You've been protecting your son his whole life, Governor. He needs you to tell the truth. Protect him this one last time," Samuel said, hoping he could push Michael Todd over the edge—Michael might be a conniving politician, but he certainly loved his son.

There was silence for a few more seconds before Samuel got his wish.

"She was threatening me," Michael said quietly. "She was accusing me of inappropriate behavior—coming on to her and whatnot. She said she was going to leak the messages I sent her. Even then I knew I was going to run for president, and she was going to blow up my campaign years before I'd even begun. What she was accusing me of… It would have ruined my marriage and my family, let alone my career!"

"Dad, no," Shep whispered, looking like he was going to pass out.

"So you'd been sending her inappropriate messages?" Maggie asked.

Everything was clicking into place for Samuel, further confirming his suspicions of the Governor. He recalled Carlie's visible discomfort in the photo where Michael had his arm around her waist and her attempts to meet up with Shep only around others and not at his house. "You were flirting with your own son's girlfriend?"

"It was harmless," Michael growled. "She was blowing it out of proportion. I stole a couple of kisses from her, sent her a few messages that wouldn't look great out of context." Even when he was cornered, Michael was unable to take accountability for his actions. Samuel felt disgust rising like bile in his throat as Michael continued talking. "I knew how it would look if she went public with all of it. So I told her I wanted to talk to her and apologize. I said we could work out a deal, that I could offer her money if she'd keep quiet. Her family was always struggling for money. I mean, her father was a no-good druggie! She agreed to come to the cabin to talk privately and she was supposed to show me evidence that she'd destroyed all the messages."

"Why did you need to meet on South Rock Island to do that?" Maggie asked, confused. "It's so convoluted."

"Because you *did* plan to kill her. It *was* premeditated," Samuel said quietly. "That's the part I got wrong. I thought it was a crime of passion, but you'd always planned to kill her. Why so violently?"

"I began to rethink my plan of paying her off. She was smart, I'll give her that, and I couldn't trust that once I'd paid her, she wouldn't keep coming after me. I couldn't have loose ends like that. I figured no one would look too hard at some dead motherless teenager from an island in the Pacific Northwest. So, I decided to kill her.

"I'd planned to drown her, but she ran. I had to chase her around that island, and I found her hiding in the cabin. There was a struggle and we ended up outside. I hit her on the head with a rock." Michael looked like he was almost in a trance now, the weight of his sin finally being shed after years. Samuel had seen it before in many interrogations—assailants who had harbored terrible secrets for years feeling almost joy as the pressure of holding on to their heinous crimes was alleviated. Samuel could see that relief in Michael Todd now, his face slackening and shoulders relaxing. "She went down so fast, I couldn't believe it. There was a lot of blood, but it was raining and most of it washed into the soil. Eventually I carried her down to the beach and left her on the rocks." He looked up. "But you said she was missing the necklace she always wore?"

"Yes," Maggie said, blinking away tears from her eyes. Samuel wished he could reach out and hold her, understanding the terrible toll these words must be taking on her.

"She must have taken it off and hidden it while she was in the cabin." Michael shrugged. "In any case, I took the boat straight here, to the chief's cabin. I knew no one would be here, so I borrowed some clothes, burned the ones I'd been wearing, and went home. No one ever guessed it was me."

There wasn't a shred of remorse in Michael's demeanor. Samuel felt confirmed in his initial profile of the man. Michael Todd was charismatic, manipulative and lacking in any empathy. He was so charming that he could hide his true intentions and actions, which made it difficult for anyone to suspect he would be involved in a murder. It was his sense of entitlement and lack of empathy for the girl he had murdered that made Samuel suspect a narcissistic personality disorder. Michael believed he was above the law and entitled to do anything he needed to protect his reputation and career.

"You've lived with this for a decade?" Samuel shook his head and let out a low whistle. "That is some serious cognitive dissonance, Governor Todd. No one suspected you. Not even your family." Samuel fixed his eyes on Shep, who was in shock next to his father, trembling and still silently crying. Michael may be a narcissist, but Shep was just a spoiled kid who'd never had the good sense to see what was right in front of him.

"Oh, come on, Shep, get a grip," Michael said, also turning to look at his son. He shook him roughly and slapped his cheek. “Don’t you realize? This was all for you! You and your mother and your sister—a family legacy. You are going to be the son of the president of the United States of America!”

“You killed my girlfriend and you expect me to be grateful?” Shep sobbed.

“I expect you to keep it together, Shepherd,” Michael said, cuffing his son on the side of the head. “You always were a spineless waste of space. I’ve done my best to drag you along, but there’s only so much I can do.” Samuel wondered whether his initial belief that Michael truly loved his son was correct. Maybe he saw Shep as an extension of himself, just one more thing that was supposed to reflect back positively on himself. The look of disdain he gave his son made Samuel almost pity Shep. Almost.

Michael turned back to face Samuel, anger and contempt oozing from his pores. “So, you have your confession, much good it will do you. What’s your next step? Because from where I’m sitting, you have a bunch of useless documents and accusations that won’t get you through the front door of a courthouse.”

“Well, that might be the case…except what I have is a *recorded* confession. And that changes everything.” Samuel enjoyed the dramatic pause, before pulling out his phone with a flourish. He looked at the screen, and saw that it was black. His phone had run out of battery.

THIRTEEN

The room was silent for a moment. Maggie stared at Samuel's screen, then at the dismayed expression on his face. Finally, Michael burst out laughing. "Wow, a dead phone! Terrifying!" He wiped tears of mirth from his eyes.

"It may be dead now, but a portion of our conversation was certainly recorded, and it's been uploaded directly to my Bureau database," Samuel said firmly. Maggie hoped the others were convinced by his bravado, but she could hear a falter in his voice.

"That's a risk I'm more than willing to take. I'm sure you've figured out by now, I have friends all over the place...including the FBI. How do you think I avoided that initial investigation, the one where your friend probably found those documents you were talking about?" Michael rolled his eyes. "It's all too easy. I have enough money and power to take care of any legal issues."

"What do you want to do with these guys?" Chief Jones walked over to stand next to the sofa. Michael stood up, ignoring his silent son. "The storm has nearly blown over and I'll need to head out to lead cleanup efforts. We have to get this done."

"I think we've played enough games." Michael pulled a handgun from his waistband. "Unfortunately, you are both about to be the victims of a tragic hunting accident." He pointed the black muzzle at Samuel, then at Maggie.

"I wouldn't do that if I were you," Maggie said, her voice quiet but firm. She stared down the barrel of the gun as if it were nothing more than a pointed finger, though her heart was pounding as if it might burst out of her chest.

"And why is that, Ms. Dalton?" Michael smiled widely. He seemed to be almost enjoying himself.

"Surely, Governor Todd, you don't think that's the only recording device we have?" Maggie crossed her arms and stared hard at him.

"You have another phone without any battery to try and scare me with?"

"Not a phone. Cameras." Maggie pointed up at the security cameras which were peeking out from the eaves of the roof, the tiny red lights blinking intermittently. "I assume Chief Jones had these put in to deter thieves? I know some of the cabins on Vargo get targeted during the offseason."

"Yeah, I put them in. The trouble with that, Ms. Dalton, is that they're *my* cameras. You aren't getting any of the footage off them," Jones said dismissively.

"Oh, I'd never trouble you with that, Chief Jones," Maggie said in an unassuming tone. "I went ahead and had a good friend of mine hack into your security system. You really shouldn't have been so cheap. Your firmware was very outdated. And hasn't anyone ever told you not to use your own birth date as a password? It took my friend about thirty seconds to break into your system and access the live footage. It's being uploaded to a secure database as we speak. Wave, everyone!" Maggie smiled and waved jauntily toward the security camera. Everett would get a kick out of that. Her editor had been only too delighted to hack into the cameras, knowing the exclusive scoop they'd capture would more than make up for any trouble that came from hacking the footage. Everett was more of an "ask for forgiveness, not permission" kind of person.

"Jones, tell me your cameras don't record sound," Michael said through gritted teeth.

"They're not the most sophisticated cameras, but I assure you, they certainly record sound," Maggie said. She looked over at Samuel, who was beaming at her with pride. She wanted to throw herself into his arms. "All this footage is being uploaded live, and my friend will be alerting the authorities as we speak. It won't take them long to get here, storm or not. If I were you, I wouldn't add another murder charge to the long list of crimes you'll be going down for."

"Shut up!" Michael lunged toward her without warning. His eyes were burning pits of hate, and strands of spit flew from between his teeth as he screamed at her. "If I'm going down, so are you."

"Get away from her!" Samuel lunged at Michael, tackling him to the floor with a hard thud. Suddenly, Jones was tripping over the flailing legs as he tried to get around to her. Maggie looked for Boyd and Thatcher, only to see them hightailing it out of the cabin. They were loyal, but only to a point. Michael Todd wasn't worth going down for murder.

In a burst of rage, Michael pushed Samuel off him and scampered up with a speed that defied his older years. He jumped up and over the coffee table between them and hooked an arm around Maggie's neck. "Everyone stop, now!" The muzzle of his gun was pressed to her temple. She could feel the sinister iciness of the metal against her skin.

"Michael, wait," Samuel said quietly, raising his hands. Maggie was reminded of him doing the exact same thing just hours ago, in the caves on South Rock Island. Somehow Michael's seething rage seemed even more threatening than Boyd and Thatcher's had been. There was a darkness that ran to Michael's core. She could feel her limbs shaking—a mixture of fear, exhaustion and hunger.

"You idiots have ruined my life," Michael hissed, desperation dripping from his words. Maggie knew that desperation would make him reckless. "I was going to be the next president, and look what you've done! All over some stupid girl who was never going to amount to anything!"

Fury built up in Maggie's chest, filling her lungs until she thought she would explode. Carlie had her whole life ahead of her. She was brilliant and wanted to study medicine. She would have helped so many people, and one selfish man ended her life to avoid the consequences of his own bad choices. Without thinking, Maggie rammed her elbow into Michael's gut and twisted her leg around his. Michael was still standing, and he sent a warning shot into the roof.

For a moment, Maggie was deafened by the discharge so close to her ear. She froze but whispered, "Carlie was going to change the world. It's you who hasn't amounted to anything."

"You really don't know when to shut up, do you?" Michael seethed, tightening his arm around her neck. He pointed the gun at Samuel, then back at Maggie's head. "If you know what's good for you, you'll stay right here. I'm getting out of here, and she's coming with me."

"Take me instead," Samuel said, terror carved into his face.

"No!" Maggie shouted. She had put him in enough danger, and if she was going to die today, she would die knowing Samuel was safe. "It's okay, Sam. Just do what Michael says."

Samuel took a step forward, and Michael fired another warning shot before placing the muzzle back against Maggie's temple. Her ears were ringing, and she had to read Samuel's lips to understand what he said next.

"I've got your back, Mags."

Michael pulled her backward with him as he retreated out of the cabin. She stared at Samuel's face, trying to memorize the fine cut of his cheekbones and the ripple of his dimples. He was so dear to her, dearer than her own life, and she wished she'd told him. She wished she'd allowed herself to be more vulnerable years ago, that she'd returned his calls when they first went to college. She wished they'd have had more time together.

So many wishes, and all for nothing.

Then they were running, Michael holding her by the scruff of her hoodie and keeping the gun raised and pointed at her. She couldn't safely break away without the risk of getting shot, so she kept pace with him. They sprinted down the same dirt path she'd followed with Samuel earlier, except this time Michael pulled her along another track that broke off from it.

The mud splashed up beneath their feet as they raced along. Maggie's breath was coming in short ragged bursts, her chest tight and feet aching. She was about to beg for a break when they emerged in a clearing, a sleek helicopter sitting right in the middle.

Michael brought her right to it and pushed her into the copilot seat toward the front. He clambered in next to her, keeping his gun trained on her.

"Don't try anything," he warned her. "I've got nothing left to lose. I'll kill you without a second thought."

"Just let me go," Maggie said, shrinking back from him in the seat. "I'm worthless to you now."

"We'll see about that," Michael muttered under his breath. He slid a headset over his ears and settled back into the seat. "Shep usually flies us, but I can handle this bird well enough for our needs." He began hitting buttons, and Maggie heard the starter motor rev up. The blades above them began to whir, readying the helicopter to ascend. She knew if they took off, her life would be in mortal danger.

She made a last attempt to escape, throwing herself toward the door, but Michael held her back. She managed to scramble into the row of passenger seats behind the pilot's chair, but it was too late. She felt the helicopter lift off the ground, and a terrible finality settled in her chest. This was it. *Lord, if this is my final moment, please be with me and keep Samuel safe.*

Suddenly, a heavy weight tilted the helicopter to one side.

Samuel took a running leap and grasped the helicopter's landing skid with all his might, his fingers closing around the cold metal as it rose higher into the sky. He was lifted from the ground with the machine, his weight forcing the helicopter to lean to one side even as it continued ascending.

Wind from the spinning rotors battered his face, his legs swinging wildly over the grassy glade below. Gritting his teeth, he tightened his grip, muscles straining as he fought against gravity. He knew Maggie was just above him, and with a determined grunt, he began to haul himself up, one desperate pull at a time.

"Maggie!" he screamed, knowing he wouldn't be heard over the sound of the rotor blades. Though it had stopped raining, his hands were beginning to sweat and he knew he couldn't hold on much longer. He swung one leg over the skid, then the other leg, trying not to think about how high they were getting. He could see the tops of the trees were now level with them.

Just as he began to fear he would be lifted even higher, the helicopter stopped its ascent, hovering just above the tips of the waving pines. The door above him opened and Michael's face appeared.

"I told you not to follow us!" he screamed at Samuel over the loud whir of the blades. Suddenly Maggie's face appeared next to him, panic gripping her features. Michael pushed her farther forward.

"Stop!" Samuel commanded.

"It's you or her!" Michael shouted back. "Either you let go, or I'll let go of her!" Michael had her by both arms, leaning her shoulders and head out of the helicopter. Her hair spun in the air around her, curls flying in every direction. He could just make out her face beneath the mass of coils, her mouth a silent *O* of horror.

What happened next seemed to be in slow motion. With a grace that belied the force of the action, Maggie reared backward. The crown of her head smashed into Michael's face, driving them both back inside the helicopter. Suddenly Michael's bloodied face reappeared, trying to pull Maggie back out again. With all the energy left in his body Samuel swung both arms through the open door, using his wrapped legs to keep him secured to the helicopter. For a heart-stopping second, he couldn't find anything to grasp. But then his hands found the steel bars beneath the bench seat.

Using his elbows for leverage, he hauled his torso up and saw Maggie and Michael grappling. Michael was trying to push her toward the open door while Maggie kicked and scratched him. Even in this moment of extreme danger, Samuel felt pure admiration for Maggie's strength and fight.

With a final, desperate heave, Samuel swung himself into the helicopter's cabin, the wind roaring around him. Michael barely had time to react before Samuel struck—fingers jabbing with pinpoint precision into the man's neck, right at the vagus nerve. Michael went rigid, a choked gasp escaping his lips before his muscles betrayed him. His hands slipped from the controls. As the helicopter wobbled in midair, Samuel seized the stick and wrestled for control while Michael slumped over, unconscious. Maggie stared in wide-eyed shock.

"Mags, are you okay?" he asked, taking his eyes off the controls for a moment to search for Michael's gun. He found it on the seat and passed it to Maggie. "Keep this pointed at him. If he moves, if he threatens us, you shoot."

"I will," she responded, sitting back on her haunches to catch her breath. "Are *you* okay? That was some movie star action there!"

"I told you I have your back!" Samuel grinned.

"So am I supposed to add 'helicopter pilot' to your list of hidden talents?" Maggie asked nervously, looking at Samuel's hands on the controls. "How are we going to land this thing?"

"I can do it," Samuel replied. He was glad he'd had some piloting practice in the early years of his Bureau training, even if it was very limited. "I just need you to keep our friend under control."

Maggie nodded, keeping her gun trained on Michael.

Samuel slid the helicopter door shut and then squeezed into the cockpit seat. "Brace yourself, this isn't going to be pretty! It's been a while since I've done anything like this."

Samuel gripped the controls in his sweat-slicked hands with white-knuckle intensity, his breath coming in short, focused bursts. The helicopter wobbled as he adjusted the collective, the skids dipping unevenly. Alarms beeped in protest and the ground loomed closer as his pulse hammered in his ears. He bit his lip, easing off the cyclic ever so slightly, fighting the jerky movements with sheer willpower. The helicopter bucked once, twice, and then it finally touched down with a shuddering jolt. The rotors whined and dust swirled around the craft as he exhaled shakily, realizing only then that he had been holding his breath.

The sudden silence as Samuel killed the engines was a welcome relief, but then he noticed shouting. He maneuvered back out into the cabin and opened the door in time to see several armed police officers approaching the helicopter.

FOURTEEN

It took several moments for the officers to allow Samuel and Maggie to step outside, but then they swarmed on Michael, cuffing him and pulling him from the helicopter. Maggie felt the warm strength of Samuel's fingers interlacing with hers, and together they stumbled to the edge of the clearing. Beneath the sheltering boughs of a pine, they turned to look at each other.

"You came for me," Maggie said breathlessly. She placed a hand on Samuel's chest, over his heart. She could feel it thudding beneath her palm, fast and true.

"I'm always going to protect you, Mags," Samuel said, placing his own hand over hers.

Maggie felt her hands trembling. The space between them felt alive, charged with years of unspoken words and distance. The noise of the sirens and police activity faded into the distance, leaving only the soft rhythm of their breathing in their perfect bubble. Their eyes met, and the past, the what-ifs, the missed moments—all of it melted away as Samuel leaned in and kissed her, as the whole world seemed to hold its breath. It was the moment she hadn't dared to hope for. Electricity coursed through her limbs, and she could feel heat radiating from him.

As the kiss ended, they looked into each other's eyes.

"I wanted to tell you. On graduation day all those years ago," Samuel said softly.

"Tell me what?" Maggie asked.

"That I love you." Samuel held both her hands in his. She could feel his thumbs tracing circles on the tops of her hands.

"Why didn't you say anything?" Maggie was breathless with hope.

"Because you had these plans to go to UCLA, big dreams and a need to get out of Vargo. I could see how much you needed that, and I guess I was plain scared to tell you. I could see how much pain you were in after Carlie's death, and I didn't want to remind you of that." Samuel stepped back from her slightly and dropped her hands.

"I'm sorry I ran," Maggie said, overcome with emotion. "I should have let you in, but I didn't know how. Everything felt so fragile after what happened to Carlie. I had trouble trusting anyone. I should have trusted you. I *do* trust you."

"I know," Samuel replied. "I think we were both scared."

"And now?" Maggie hardly dared ask. She could feel laughter bubbling up in her throat at the absurdity of the situation they found themselves in. She felt as though she were dreaming.

"I'm not scared anymore." Samuel dropped to one knee and held one of her hands, his fingers trembling slightly despite the certainty in his gaze. Her laughter caught in her throat, her eyes widening as realization dawned.

"Margaret Dalton, I love you. We've let ten years go by without saying that to each other, and now I don't want to go another day. I want to say it every day for the rest of our lives," Samuel said, his voice thick with emotion. "Mags, will you marry me?"

Maggie's hands flew to her mouth, tears collecting in the corners of her eyes, as the weight of the moment wrapped around them both. She only needed a second to respond.

"Yes." She was crying so hard that she could barely choke the word out. Samuel's crooked grin of delight made her cry even more. He stood up, cupped her face with both his hands and kissed her again with an intensity that had been building for over a decade.

Their lips parted and they embraced. Maggie rested her forehead in the crook of his neck, breathing in his scent. "I love you, too, Samuel Reyes." She repeated the words over and over, delighting in their sound. She could hear his laughter deep within his chest. She stepped back.

"So now what?" Maggie asked.

"What do you mean?" Samuel looped an arm around her shoulders, and they began walking toward the cluster of officers who were standing in the clearing.

"Exactly that… What's next for us?"

"I was thinking—we make a pretty good team," Samuel said, squeezing her shoulders. "I think we should keep this going. What if we form our own little cold case squad? We could investigate cold cases the police have given up on, and you can write about the experiences."

"You know, I think that could work," Maggie mused. Excitement swelled within her. "As long as we have each other's backs, it will all work out."

EPILOGUE

FIFTEEN MONTHS LATER

Maggie gazed at her reflection in the full-length mirror, taking in the woman staring back at her. For the first time in years, she wasn't running—from grief, from fear, from the past. Nor was she frantically planning for the future, worrying about her next byline or case. Instead, she was completely in the present. She stood in utter contentment and silently prayed.

Lord, thank You for the gift of this moment. Thank You for accompanying me and guiding me. Please be at my side as I take this next step.

She ran her hands over the embroidery of her wedding gown, understated and elegant, just as she'd always hoped. She took in the breathtaking details—from the square neckline to the structured bodice to the sheer back panel studded with delicate pearl buttons. A slow smile spread across her lips. *This is really happening,* she thought to herself.

She touched the empty space around her collarbone where her friendship necklace normally sat. In the rush of the morning she'd completely forgotten to bring it with her to get changed at the church.

A quiet knock at the door pulled her from her thoughts. "Come in," she called, already knowing who it would be.

Everett peeked her head in, a teasing grin on her face. "You ready, Dalton? It's almost time." She had been her editor up until recently, and Maggie was grateful she could still call her a friend and, today, her maid of honor. Everett's short, practical haircut matched her simple gray pantsuit—when Maggie had said she could wear anything to the wedding, Everett had taken that to heart.

"I think so," she said, though her heart pounded not with doubt, but with the enormity of the moment. "Thank you, again, for being here. I know driving up from Los Angeles when you're so busy is—"

"Will you stop? There's nowhere else I'd want to be!" Everett cried, cutting her off. She stepped into the room fully, her eyes warm with pride. "I have to say, I never pictured you settling down in a tiny island town. But then again, I never pictured you taking down a political dynasty, either. So I guess you're just full of surprises!"

Maggie smiled, thinking back to everything that had happened in the past fifteen months. After Samuel had rescued her from the helicopter, Michael Todd had been arrested for murder, attempted kidnapping and fraud. He was sentenced to life in prison without the possibility of parole, a shocking downfall for the governor. Chief Jones, Boyd and Thatcher were likewise arrested and sentenced to multiyear prison sentences. Joey was given a reduced sentence because of his cooperation with authorities and Samuel's testimony that he had tried to help them.

Most importantly, Carlie's death had been reinvestigated and officially ruled a homicide. Michael Todd had thought he was untouchable, but because of Maggie and Samuel's tenacity, he was finally facing the consequences of his actions. It was bittersweet—too late to save Carlie's life, but at least the truth had been revealed.

Maggie and Samuel hadn't stopped at Michael Todd's arrest. Together, they had built something more than just a life together—they had built a purpose. Using Maggie's investigative skills and Samuel's experience in criminal profiling, they had founded a cold case investigative team, working with journalists and law enforcement agencies to bring long-forgotten cases back into the light. Some days were frustrating, the work slow and painstaking. But every solved case, every grieving family given closure, made it worth it.

Maggie had slowly begun moving her life back up to Vargo.

She lived on the mainland, traveling most days to help Samuel further renovate his cabin in preparation for when she moved in after the wedding. Samuel had added a bright new office to the cabin, brimming with files on cold cases they would be working on. They'd also begun building an extra room—they weren't in a rush, but they both wanted a family someday soon.

A gust of wind rattled the window, drawing her attention to the view outside. Through the thin lace curtains that adorned the church windows, she could see the bay stretching endlessly toward the horizon. Today the weather was perfect, the sun glinting like millions of diamonds over the waves. It seemed a world away from that stormy day when they'd discovered the truth on South Rock Island, where the dark waters had threatened their lives.

There was a knock at the door. Maggie turned toward it, smiling as Samuel's deep voice floated into the room. "Is it breaking tradition to see the bride before the wedding?"

"Yes!" Maggie laughed, though she didn't really believe this. They'd had a very unconventional path to finding each other. Their love transcended conventions. "But I'll make an exception for you."

Everett grinned. "I'll leave you to it," she said, slipping out the door as Samuel stepped inside.

Samuel leaned against the doorframe, his immaculate suit perfectly tailored, his eyes dark and warm. The sight of him made her breath catch. She seemed to have had the same effect on him. He cleared his throat and rubbed his eyes, clearly brushing away tears, before meeting her gaze again.

"Mags...you are perfect," he said softly. She smiled at him, her heart full to bursting. She noticed a spray of flowers on his lapel.

"I thought you were going to wear a rose boutonniere?" Maggie asked.

"Last-minute change. These are forget-me-nots...for Carlie," he said, and Maggie had to press her eyes closed to stop from crying and ruining her makeup.

"*That* is perfect," Maggie whispered after a moment.

"Speaking of Carlie... I think you're forgetting something." Samuel stepped up to her, and in his outstretched hand she saw the coil of a gold necklace. Her friendship necklace. Wordlessly, she turned so he could drape the chain around her neck and fasten it at the back. She turned around again, looking at her reflection and touching the heart.

In the mirror, she watched as Samuel kissed the back of her head and put his hands on her shoulders. "Are you sure you still want to do this?" he teased, but there was a softness in his voice.

Maggie smiled, reaching up to squeeze his hands. "I've never been more sure of anything. We've got each other's backs, right?" As she walked down the aisle toward Samuel a few moments later, she knew for sure—she had finally found her truth.

* * * * *

Dear Reader,

From the moment the idea for this story sparked in my mind, I knew it would be about resilience, redemption and the power of confronting the past. I was inspired by the concept of unfinished business—how unresolved grief and guilt can shape a person's life, pushing them toward or away from the truth.

Maggie Dalton is a woman who has spent a decade running—from her past, from her regrets and from the person she once was. Writing her journey showed me how courage is not about fearlessness but about standing firm *despite* fear. Samuel Reyes, on the other hand, has spent his life protecting others, but he's never been able to save the person who mattered most. Together, their journey taught me that healing and redemption are often found in the search for truth.

I hope you enjoy uncovering the secrets of Vargo Island alongside Maggie and Samuel. Thank you for being a part of this story.

Warmly,
Leah Conte